The Earl to be In Disguise

An Enemies to Lovers Sweet Regency Romance

Kerri Kastle

Kerri Kastle Books

Copyright © 2025 by Kerri Kastle

All rights reserved.

No portion of this book may be reproduced in any form without written permission from the publisher or author, except as permitted by U.S. copyright law.

Contents

Prologue		1
1.	Chapter One	5
2.	Chapter Two	13
3.	Chapter Three	22
4.	Chapter Four	31
5.	Chapter Five	38
6.	Chapter Six	45
7.	Chapter Seven	53
8.	Chapter Eight	62
9.	Chapter Nine	69
10.	Chapter Ten	77
11.	Chapter Eleven	85
12.	Chapter Twelve	93
13.	Chapter Thirteen	101

14.	Chapter Fourteen	110
15.	Chapter Fifteen	119
16.	Chapter Sixteen	127
17.	Chapter Seventeen	136
18.	Chapter Eighteen	145
19.	Chapter Nineteen	155
20.	Chapter Twenty	172
21.	Chapter Twenty-One	181
22.	Chapter Twenty-Two	189
23.	Chapter Twenty-Three	196
24.	Chapter Twenty-Four	205
25.	Chapter Twenty-Five	214
	Epilogue	221

Prologue

April 1814, Worsley Manor, Buckinghamshire, England

"I think she's waking up, Sir Henry!" Abby heard her brother Ralph exclaim softly nearby, relief in his voice. "That's good, isn't it?"

Abby surfaced from the darkness, aware of excruciating pain in her head and upper body, and soft amber light that flickered as large shadows moved within its glow.

"Yes, it's good. However, it remains to be seen how she'll take the bad news. It will be a terrible shock. She could very well swoon," replied a deep, sonorous voice gravely. Abby recognized it immediately.

Sir Henry Porton? But what is the physician doing here? What is he talking about? Bad news? Is someone hurt?

She opened her eyes, her vision swimming as she struggled to make out where she was and confirm the identity of the two tall figures standing over her. Glancing upwards in confusion, she saw the familiar canopy of her bed and realized she was in her chambers.

What am I doing here? Is this a dream?

"I'll tell her, if you don't mind, Sir Henry," Ralph said. "I think she'll take it best from me." Her brother's face, drawn and tired, swam into focus as he leaned over her, partially blocking out what she now realized was lamplight.

Take what?

Trying to find her voice to ask all the questions crowding in on her, Abby swallowed painfully. Her throat felt like sandpaper, and the unpleasant acrid smell of burning lingered in her nostrils.

"Ralph?" she said, surprised at the harsh croak that came out of her mouth. She reached for his hand, seeking comfort. The side of the bed dipped as he sat next to her and took her hand in his. She gripped it tightly, reassured. "What has happened? Why am I here?" she asked, growing anxious because of the distraught expression on his face.

His brows knitted, and, though he smiled at her fondly, she could see something was very wrong. "Hello, Sister, I'm so glad to see you're awake. You had me worried for a while," he told her softly, squeezing her fingers. "You're in your bedroom, Abby, darling. You had an accident and hurt yourself. Sir Henry has come to help you."

Abby frowned and tried to push herself up on her elbows. Instantly, agony tore through her, and she let out a small scream as she fell back onto the pillow. Never knowing such pain, panic seized her. "What is this pain? What has happened to me?" she gasped, every movement torture.

The familiar be-whiskered, ruddy face of Sir Henry appeared over Ralph's shoulder. "It is best that you lie completely still, Lady Lucas. You have sustained some nasty burns to your left shoulder, arm, and neck," the usually brusque old physician said not unkindly.

"Burns? But how— Oh!"

She broke off as the shocking memories flooded into her mind, a rushing tide of images of being asleep in her bed and then suddenly waking to the frantic neighing of panicked horses, of throwing open the window and smelling smoke, of rushing outside in a panic in her nightclothes, reliving the horror of seeing the stables on fire, hearing the terrified screams of the trapped horses.

An alarm bell clanged distantly at the back of her mind. *Help is coming*, she had told herself, *but not soon enough. I have to get the horses out! I have to save them!*

She recalled plunging into the smoke-filled building, heedless of the flames hungrily consuming the roof timbers, covering her mouth and nose with her arms as she hurriedly opened every stall and began urging the horses outside.

"The fire! I remember it now," she croaked before voicing her immediate thought, "Are the horses all right? I tried my best to get them to safety."

Ralph patted her hand. "They're all fine, thanks to your brave action, darling," he told her soothingly. "And the fire was put out before the whole stable block could be destroyed." He explained how one of the young grooms asleep in the loft had accidentally knocked over a candlestick and panicked as the flames took hold.

"Is he all right? Was anyone else hurt?" Abby asked, shaken afresh by the ordeal.

Ralph's face crumpled alarmingly. He shook his head and replied, "No, no one else was hurt. Only you, dear sister. Do you remember? A burning timber fell on you and knocked you out. I'm afraid you were quite badly burned before we could get it off of you and pull you clear."

Abby breathed a sigh of relief that the horses were safe and there was no more harm done. "I don't remember being knocked out," she admitted, coming up blank. "But I certainly feel the burns." With her other hand, she softly touched the tight bandaging that stretched across the left-hand side of her upper body, up her shoulder and the side of her neck beneath her nightdress. "It feels like I'm still on fire," she said, wincing as fresh agony shot through her.

"The pain will be bad for some time, I'm afraid, Lady Abby. I shall give you some medicine to help ease it and to sleep. That is the best thing for you now: sleep and rest. You shall make a full recovery in time, I assure you," the physician told her with a kind smile.

Abby detected the pitying note in his voice and saw the uneasy glance her brother and the physician shared. An icicle entered her heart like a little dagger as Ralph's earlier words came back to her: *"I'll tell her, if you don't mind, Sir Henry,"* he had said. *"I think she'll take it best from me."*

"Thank you for your help, Sir Henry, I am very grateful to you. But I see you have something else to tell me. What is it?"

The physician cleared his throat awkwardly and stepped away from the bed. Ralph shifted closer to her and held her hand more tightly, looking sadly into her eyes. Abby looked back at him, holding her breath, dreading confirmation of what she already suspected.

"It's the burns, Abby. Sir Henry says they have gone deep. They'll heal in time, and you shall be as good as new. But there will be scarring of the skin, I'm afraid, severe scarring that will remain with you for the rest of your life."

It was at that moment when Sir Henry's prediction came true, for Abby felt suddenly dizzy. The chamber began to swirl about her, and darkness pooled at the edges of her vision ... until finally, mercifully, it swallowed everything.

Chapter One

May 1817, near Beaconsfield, Buckinghamshire, England

"Worsley House." Damian Ross said aloud as he looked out of the carriage window and read the name carved in capitals into the grand stone piers flanking a set of massive wrought iron gates. "Yes, this is it," he shouted up to the driver of the hired cab. "Take me up to the house."

He stuck his head out of the open window as they drove up a long, winding drive, admiring the spectacular countryside. "Perfect horse country," he murmured to himself with a satisfied smile, thinking how much he was going to enjoy living amongst it.

"Oh, what is that?" he murmured, suddenly distracted by a flash of scarlet atop one of the distant hills. Squinting against the sun, he made out a galloping rider standing up in the stirrups, urging the horse to go faster. The pair raced along the ridge, sharply silhouetted against the expanse of blue sky.

Filled with curiosity, he quickly pulled from his coat pocket a small spyglass, which he habitually used to study equine form in motion from afar. Craning his neck to keep horse and rider in view despite the moving vehicle, he eagerly fixed the scarlet rider in his sights.

"Oh, I say!" he exclaimed, his breath stolen away by the vision he could now see clearly as though it were only a few feet away. *A woman! But she's riding astride, like a man. How scandalous!*

And what a woman she appeared to be, with a finely carved profile, long dark hair blowing out behind her, and a flurry of crimson skirts about her legs as she leaned forward in the saddle and flew across the ridge.

"Well, whoever she is, she has a fine seat," he murmured, quite entranced by the lady's skill in the saddle as well as her striking looks. "Blast it, she's disappeared," he added in frustration as she passed from view.

But he quickly chided himself for his curiosity. *No, I shall not ask Ralph who she is. Beautiful she may be, but she can be of no interest to me. No romantic entanglements, that is what I have promised myself. I am here for the business, that is all.*

Accordingly, he stowed the intriguing vision away with his spyglass just as the carriage swung around and pulled up in front of an ancient, sprawling manor house that nestled in well-manicured gardens.

He alighted from the cab, his boots crunching on gravel, grateful to stretch his long limbs after the tedious journey. Surrounded by tranquility and birdsong, breathing sweetly-scented summer air, he took off his hat and paused to admire the picturesque old building in front of him.

Constructed in the Elizabethan style of red brick and black timber, the manor's walls had been mellowed by time to a soft, ruddy amber. The old place looked inviting.

Damian nodded to himself. "I think I shall like it here," he mused, letting the excitement of the new adventure he was about to enter into wash over him.

After telling the cab driver to await instructions, he was about to mount the steps to the ancient porch and ring the bell when the pair of stout oak doors flew open. He looked up to see the tall, gangling frame of his old friend Ralph Lucas on the threshold, his familiar, bearded face lit by a grin.

"Damian, old man, you've arrived at last!" Ralph greeted him enthusiastically, running down the steps to seize Damian's hand and pump it vigorously. "Welcome to my humble abode, I've been dying to see you. Come along in, dear fellow."

They exchanged pleasantries as Ralph ushered him through the doors and into a large, comfortably furnished living chamber, clearly the original great hall of the manor. "You must be tired after your journey. A glass of claret will set you up, I'll wager," his host said.

Before Damian could reply, a distinguished looking, gray-haired butler appeared next to them.

"Oh, this is Withers, by the way," Ralph said, gesturing absently at the man. "If you need anything, just let him know and he'll get it for you."

"Good day to you, sir," Withers greeted Damian, bowing respectfully. "May I take your things for you?"

"Thank you," Damian answered, handing over his coat, hat, and stick, which were duly whisked away to the nearby stand.

Ralph led Damian further into the spacious hall, where sunlight lanced through the windows to illuminate the pleasantly cool interior. He gestured for Damian to make himself comfortable on a large red settee near a vast, unlit hearth. While Damian settled himself, Ralph crossed to an imposing gothic-looking sideboard and poured them both a glass of dark purple claret. On his return, he handed one to Damian before throwing himself languidly onto the sofa opposite, this one upholstered in blue brocade.

"Hungry?" he inquired.

Damian sipped the claret appreciatively. "Hmm, peckish," he admitted. "In my haste to get here as early as possible, I didn't bother stopping for luncheon."

"Hear that, Withers?" Ralph asked the lingering butler.

"Refreshments coming right away, Milord," Withers replied before pulling on a bell rope and abruptly vanishing.

"What a nice place you have here, Ralph. I wonder why you haven't asked me to visit before."

"Can't have any old riff raff rolling up, can I?" Ralph joked in response. "What would the neighbors think?"

"But you have need of me now, I suppose. How mercenary of you. Joking aside, I must say, I'm very excited about this new venture. Are we truly to be partners?"

"Of course! I have the papers all drawn up, ready to sign. You can have a good read of them tonight or send them to your man to be looked over. No hurry. There's fifty-fifty shares of all the profits for each of us, including prize money—when you train that Derby winner for me as promised."

Damian laughed. "Well, I've already had some success training three winners, so why not a Derby winner? I have the feeling I shall work all the harder when the profits are coming to me instead of some other old fellow who's footing the bill."

"You refer to Lord Hinkley, I'm guessing. I gather from your letters that you weren't very happy in his employ."

"That is an understatement. What he knows about horses, apart from betting his fortune backing losers at the races, can be written on the back of a postage stamp. Your invitation couldn't have come at a better time."

"I'm so glad you were unhappy. Hinkley's loss is my gain, all right. I can't wait to get started. You shall be the resident expert and have a free hand, whilst I shall simply take the credit and bask in the glory I'm confident you shall create. By the way, I've already set aside a considerable sum to purchase a couple of promising new nags to start off with. I thought we could go together to the horse fair at Stoughton next week and select them."

"Marvellous. I look forward to it," Damian replied, glad to hear their plans were already moving ahead nicely.

Refreshments duly arrived, and the two friends set about the small feast of sandwiches and cakes with enthusiasm.

"Now, how are things with you and your father at the moment? Still not made up?" Ralph enquired before stuffing a sandwich into his mouth. The pair regularly corresponded, so he was well acquainted with Damian's ongoing family drama.

Damian scowled and paused to wipe his lips with a napkin before complaining, "Did you have to bring him into it while I'm eating? No, we have certainly not made up, and I have no intention of going anywhere near him until he sees sense and sends that grasping harridan packing."

He was referring to his father's second wife, the much younger Lady Mariah, whose passion to be *à la mode* in all things had been whittling away at the Ross family fortunes at an alarming rate for the last four years. She was responsible for the row that had made Damian decide to split from his father almost eighteen months before.

"Still got her claws into him, has she?" Ralph commiserated.

"Like a bird of prey, old man. And the silly old fool loves it. He won't listen to sense. I'm sad to say so because I'm fond of him. I worry about him, but he's lost my respect. I'm better off as I am, making my own way in the world." He ate a sugared sponge finger, finding solace in its sweet crunch.

"But what about when he croaks? God forbid, I mean, but you're the son and heir. What about the earldom? Do you seriously intend to give all that up?" Ralph asked, topping up their cups from the teapot.

"Honestly, Ralph, I just don't know what will happen. But I do know how much I'm enjoying not having that responsibility hanging over me. I like being independent and carefree. Plain old Mr. Ross suits me better than Lord Ross, the Viscount Amberley, at least while that vixen still holds sway at Chartringham," Damian replied, mentioning his ancestral seat.

Ralph picked up an iced finger. "Let us hope her downfall comes soon. I should hate to see you lose your father and your birthright over such a vulgar person," he said before demolishing the cake in one bite.

"By the way," Damian went on, remembering something important. "I hear rumors that Father's looking for me, and I do not wish to be found. I hope you'll oblige me by keeping my true identity to yourself."

"Oh? So, it really is to be plain old Mr. Ross, then?"

"The common or garden variety," Damian confirmed with a nod. "Besides that, it just makes things so much easier in the horse business. If people find out I'm a noble, there'll be bowing and scraping and the usual obsequious lies. I don't want that. It would interfere with the work. So, keep it to yourself if you please."

"Nothing easier, old friend. Consider it done."

"Splendid."

"I shan't even tell my sister."

"You have a sister?" Damian asked, surprised. But then it came to him. "Oh, yes. I dimly recall you mentioning her. But she's young, is she not?" He imagined a twelve-year-old in a pinny with plaits.

Ralph snorted. "You're several years out of date, old chap. Abby's twenty-six now."

Twenty-six?

He felt a flicker of unease. "Is she, by God? Time flies, eh? I suppose she's betrothed then or married, is she?" he asked hopefully.

Ralph shook his head as he chewed on a jam tart. "Single."

Twenty-six and still single? That's old maid territory!

Damian coughed as a currant went down the wrong way. Ralph shoved his teacup at him, urging him to drink. He drank, dislodging the rogue currant, thinking, *Lord, I hope this sister of his isn't the bossy, pushy type desperate to bag a husband.*

Such had been his, unpleasant, experience of women of the *Ton* so far, and he fervently wanted to avoid any such occurrences in future. He had hated being seen as an eligible "commodity" by ambitious young women who fancied being a rich countess. With that and his troublesome stepmother to boot, his attitude to romance and matrimony were jaded to say the least. He had utterly sworn off any entanglement for the foreseeable future.

But I mustn't prejudge the lady unfairly before I meet her, he told himself, trying to put his fears aside and focus instead on the prospect of building the business.

"Yes, Abby is a fine horsewoman and passionate about horses," Ralph went on cheerfully, oblivious to Damian's worries. "She practically lives at the stables."

Oh, God help me. That's all I need, some interfering woman poking her nose in. "Indeed? Well, I look forward to meeting her," he fibbed.

Ralph looked sheepishly at him. "Um, well, there's one thing you should know, old chap. I haven't told her about you yet."

Damian's fears for the safety of his continuing bachelorhood rose. "What? Whyever not?"

"Well, she's not fond of strangers, you see. She's a little reclusive, likes the quiet country life, not keen on the old social whirl of the *Ton* and all that."

Damian almost dropped his tea cup in shock. *A woman who is not fond of the Season? Why, what on earth is wrong with her?*

A door banged above, and he detected light footsteps descending a staircase out of sight.

"Oh, that sounds like Abby now," Ralph said, glancing at a door at the far end of the hall. Filled with unease, Damian followed his host's gaze as he added, "How fortunate. You can meet her now instead."

Chapter Two

Invigorated by her ride across the hills, Abby was humming a merry little tune to herself as she tripped down the staircase, across the narrow hallway, and opened the door to the great room.

"Hello, Brother. Is there tea?" she inquired, gaily stepping over the threshold. "I'm absolutely parch— Oh!"

She stopped dead in her tracks, confounded by what she saw in front of her. She blinked, but when she opened her eyes, it was still there. A strange man was seated with his back to her on her favorite settee.

The moment she realized he was real and not the product of her imagination, her heart lurched painfully in her chest and then started racing. A wave of freezing anxiety washed over her body, while at the same time, her face felt like it was on fire.

She stood frozen, with her hand still on the door knob, staring at the back of the stranger's head in shock.

Why on earth has Ralph not warned me about this visitor?

"Come in, come in, Abby. There's someone I want you to meet," Ralph said with a jovial smile, getting up and gesturing with his arm for her to approach.

Silently, behind the stranger's back, she made an angry face at her brother, berating him with her eyes for not warning her about the visitor so she could avoid him.

"I apologize for springing this on you, dear," Ralph went on, deliberately ignoring her furious expression and waving her closer. The stranger moved to rise, and she knew with sinking heart that it was too late to flee, that she would somehow have to face him.

As the man stood up, she noticed he was a little taller than Ralph, his broad shoulders filling out his plain, dark coat like a second skin, and a mop of somewhat unruly dark hair. Despite her shock and nervousness, she thought him imposing.

When he turned to face her and she found herself looking into a pair of sparkling, bright green eyes, another jolt of shock went through, greater than the last. It shook her to her core.

She knew she was staring but found herself quite unable to look away. He was by far the handsomest man she had ever laid eyes on.

Something she could not name flitted across the handsome stranger's eyes as he maintained their gaze. The air seemed to crackle between them.

"Damian, this is my sister, Abby," Ralph said. "Abby, meet my old friend Damian Ross. I'm sure you've heard me speak of him."

Her mind a blank, Abby began to tremble as Damian Ross approached her, a tense smile on his handsome face. Barely resisting the urge to pick up her skirts and run from the room, she glanced at Ralph, who nodded at her encouragingly.

Still angry with him but anxious not to make a fool of herself, she fought to keep her composure. Braving the interloper's gaze once more, she held out her hand, praying he would not notice how it was shaking.

"H-how do y-you do, Mr. Ross?" she murmured, hating the stutter in her voice, horribly conscious of her flushing cheeks.

He bowed elegantly and kissed her hand. This time, the brief touch sparked a pleasant tingling sensation that rippled up Abby's arm. His obvious surprise as he withdrew his hand had her wondering if he might have felt it too.

"Good day to you, Lady Abby. It is a pleasure to make your acquaintance."

The sound of his deep, pleasantly husky voice seemed to resonate within her body, turning her insides to water. She had never felt anything like it before. And it was deeply unsettling.

"Likewise," she murmured, glad to have her hand back. Now she had done her duty, she wanted to get away as fast as she could, secretly hoping he would soon leave. "If you will excuse me, I shall, um, I will go and ... I have some things to do," she said, turning to leave.

"Oh, stay if you would, Abby, I need to speak to you about something important," Ralph told her hurriedly, tugging on a bell rope by the hearth. He turned to Mr. Ross, who was loitering nearby, hands clasped behind his back, looking bemused. "I'll get Withers to show you to your chambers, old chap. I trust you'll be comfortable. Now you're going to be living with us, I want you to feel like part of the family."

Abby almost fainted. *Living with us?*

She had to wait several agonizing minutes, pasting on a smile, hiding her nausea, enduring their jocular banter, before Withers arrived to escort Mr. Ross to wherever he was going to be staying, leaving her the opportunity to speak her mind to her brother.

When the door closed upon the butler and Mr. Ross, after their footsteps had faded from earshot, she wheeled on Ralph.

"Living with us? Part of the family? Just what is it you've been plotting behind my back, Ralph?!" she demanded, unleashing her anger at last.

"I'm sorry. I wanted to tell you, Abby," he admitted, shrugging sheepishly, hands in pockets, "but knowing how you hate people coming here, well, I kept putting it off."

"So, you thought it would be better to spring it on me like this, did you? You let me walk in here without warning me about a visitor. It is clear to me that you planned it this way. You deliberately waited until Mr. Ross' arrival was a *fait accompli*, knowing that however much fuss I made, I would have to accept it or appear outright rude," she accused him, terrified at the thought of having to share her home with the disturbingly handsome stranger.

"Nonsense!" Ralph said indignantly. "You should know I would never do such a thing. I just ... ran out of time, that is all." He approached her, palms out. "Abby, I know you are afraid of being judged, but Damian is a good fellow. He's my partner now, and he believes we can make a go of this new horse business. It will be a good source of extra income for the estate."

Abby glowered at him as he paced about for a few moments, seemingly searching for inspiration. Apparently finding it, he turned to face her. "We'll invest most of the profits back into the business, of course," he told her persuasively." "But I was thinking we could channel some of them into your scheme for refurbishing the tenants' cottages. You've been planning that for ages, haven't you? Well, this will ensure the funds."

"That is an out-and-out bribe, Ralph," Abby shot back, the offer giving her pause before her anger at his betrayal made her reject it.

"How dare you! You have done the worst thing possible for my happiness by inviting that man to stay. You have schemed behind my back, without any consultation with me."

"You are making it sound so calculating, Abby. It wasn't like that at all," Ralph replied. He sounded so pained that, amid her hurt and anger, Abby felt a twinge of guilt. Her brother was her everything. She did not know how she would have endured the past four years without him to rely on. Ralph was her rock, and she always felt bad that he sacrificed his own social life for her benefit.

"All right. I forgive you!" she cried. "I do not argue with your business plan. If you recall, it was I who first mentioned the possibility of starting such a business venture to you nearly two years ago, shortly after Father died."

"You did indeed, Sister dear. And I thought it was a jolly good idea, so I'm now making it a reality, for all our benefit. So, all is well, and there's nothing to be so angry about, is there?"

"Ralph!" she cried with angry impatience. "You are insufferable. Forget your schemes for a minute and tell me why Mr. Ross is here, and why you say he is to become "part of the family." By which I understand you expect me to do the very thing you know I hate most—live under the same roof with a complete stranger and engage in daily discourse with him?!"

She knew she was babbling and being what any sane person would regard as unreasonable. But she was so agitated by the prospect of having Mr. Ross at Worsley day in, day out, she could not seem to help it.

"I have partnered with Damian because he is a trusted friend who is willingly investing his own money in the business, as well as having an excellent reputation as a stud manager and trainer. He is the best person to make the venture a success in the long-term," Ralph replied with infuriating calm, going on to give a brief outline of Mr. Ross' supposed expertise and successes in the horse racing business.

His words were like gall to Abby. "You mean to say you have given this man the role you knew was to be mine?" she demanded, shocked and hurt. "How could you, Ralph? This is the final insult in all this."

"Abby, I do not wish to hurt your feelings, but you must understand that would not work. I do not deny your knowledge of horseflesh is first rate, but you are shy of people. One cannot hope to make the business a success if one cannot deal with all sorts of people all the time. Damian can handle all that easily. I know you must be disappointed, but you will still have your horses to care for, and I'm sure there'll be a quieter role for you to play once the venture is up and running."

A quieter role? Abby held back bitter tears of frustration and disappointment. Hard truth twisted like a knife in her heart, leaving her once more contemplating the ruin of her life. Still, she could not quite swallow the bitter pill of acceptance. "But why does he have to stay here in the house? Can't you give him a cottage on the estate somewhere, so I have at least a chance of avoiding him?"

Ralph snorted in obvious bemusement. "My business partner? A peasant's cottage on the estate? I think not, Abby." He rested his hands on her shoulders and looked at her so affectionately, her heart clenched. "I know this is hard for you, but I need your cooperation in this matter. I've known Damian for years. He's a trusted friend and a good fellow. You have nothing to fear from him, I assure you. Besides, he'll be too busy to get in your way. Worsley is a big place, you know."

"I'm sure he will be busy, having stolen my life," she replied sharply as the pill finally went down, adding to her lingering nausea. "You have given me no choice in the matter. As I said, it is a *fait accompli*. I am forced to comply."

"Abby ... you silly goose," Ralph responded gently.

"No, say no more, Brother! My feelings clearly mean nothing to you. Being a man, your word is, of course, as good as the law, and you have decided I must tolerate Mr. Ross living in my home. And so I shall."

Covering her growing panic with a sarcastic glance thrown his way, she gathered her skirts and bustled to the door. At the last moment, she paused, hand on the doorknob, to fire her parting shot over her shoulder before sweeping from the room.

"But that does not mean I have to like it."

* * *

"Do not bother laying out my dinner gown, Maude. I shall dine in my room. I simply cannot face this ... this strange man across the dinner table," a deeply disturbed Abby told Maude, her lady's maid, later that evening in her chambers.

"But, Milady, if the gentleman is going to be living here at Worsley, does that mean you'll be taking all your meals alone in your chambers from now on?" the maid asked, continuing to bustle between the wardrobe and the bed, laying out fresh clothing.

"Oh, I didn't ... I haven't, oh, I don't know!" Abby replied defensively, her stomach lurching as the far-reaching impact of Mr. Ross's invasion of the safe sanctuary of her home sank in.

"I fear you won't be able to avoid him forever, Milady," Maude continued in a sensible tone whilst selecting a pale blue, high-necked dress with three-quarter sleeves from the wardrobe and hanging it on the door. "After all, if he's the master's friend, then he must be a gentleman and too polite to stare or make rude comments as you fear. Besides, I shall take especial care to cover your scars, so he will see only your beauty."

"Oh, Maude, please do not try to flatter me with such nonsense at such a time!" Abby cried out, her anxiety making her pettish.

"Milady, you are beautiful, even if you cannot see it yourself," Maude insisted gently with a long-suffering air as she smoothed the skirts of the blue gown. "I mean only to suggest that if you could find the strength to dine with the gentleman tonight, and he behaves nicely, then you might soon get used to him being about the place and lose your nervousness. And if it makes the master happy, then …" She gave a little shrug, the meaning of which was not lost on Abby.

"Now *you* are trying to bribe me! Of course, I want to please my brother, but he's asking too much!"

"He is but one gentleman, Milady, not the entire *Ton*. Young Ellen took in their refreshments earlier, and she says he's very handsome and charming. She was quite smitten."

For some unknown reason, that annoyed Abby, and she tutted. "Has she nothing better to do than concern herself with spreading idle gossip?"

Maude stopped what she was doing, looked at her mistress with sympathy, and said, "Mr. Ross is a stranger here at Worsley, Milady. The master clearly wishes him to be made welcome. If the lady of the house refuses to dine with him, then he won't feel very welcome at all, will he?"

Abby squirmed in her seat. "Oh, very well, I suppose I must do it," she finally agreed with huge reluctance, seeing no way out of it.

Maude smiled. "Good. That's the spirit, Milady." She gestured to the blue dress. "Now, I think this gown will be perfect. The net fichu helps with concealing your scars, and I'll do your hair in ringlets on your left side, to complete the effect."

Feeling like a lamb about to attend its own slaughter, Abby submitted to the maid's ministrations and dressed for dinner, inwardly steeling herself for the coming ordeal.

Chapter Three

The dining room clock chimed seven-thirty, the dinner hour. Damian, glass of wine in hand, stood next to Ralph and watched his friend glancing uneasily at the clock as the minutes ticked away.

"She's not usually so late," Ralph said with an apologetic frown, his eyes once again going to the door where his sister should enter. *If she's coming.* "She hasn't sent to say she's unwell, so I'm sure there must be a good reason for the delay."

"I'm sure there must be," Damian agreed, unable to help keep glancing at the door as well. He was secretly buzzing with excitement, impatient to come face to face with Lady Abby again. *The way she made me feel, was it a fluke?* he wondered. *Or will I be drawn to her like before?*

He was glad she could have no inkling of how she had affected him during their brief encounter that afternoon. Surprise was not in it. He had never felt anything like the powerful jolt of attraction which lanced through when he first locked eyes with the stunning, auburn-haired young woman in front of him.

The most beautiful woman I've ever seen, he recalled thinking, temporarily lost in her beautiful, light-gray eyes. They were cold and, more confusingly, full of fear. *What is it about me she finds so frightening?*

Instantly, he had recognized her as the scarlet rider, and it had been another shock to find out this was the sister his friend had just been telling him about. *And she's even more ravishingly beautiful close-up than I could have imagined.*

When their gazes had locked, he had somehow known with sinking heart that he would never get those sparkling, silvery-gray orbs out of his mind if he stayed a bachelor all his life, as he reminded himself he had sworn to do.

Lady Abby Lucas's pale oval face and softly rounded cheeks, so becomingly flushed bright pink to match her full lips, framed by her luxurious, dark auburn hair, had all pulled at him as though he were a hapless trout snagged by a fisherman's hook and being reeled in.

Warning bells had rung in his head and his face went hot as he bowed to kiss her hand in greeting. When his lips had touched the back of her lace glove, he felt it again, the same jolt as before. It radiated from her touch and ran tingling up his arm, stoking his excitement. The attraction was magnetically powerful, like nothing he had ever experienced. And it had both fascinated and terrified him.

No! No matter how lovely she is, he had lectured himself sternly, *she's twenty-six and single, an old maid by anyone's standards. If I give her a hint of encouragement, she'll set her cap at me, and I shall be lost. I have invested much in making this business with Ralph a success. I shall not allow myself to be distracted by a pretty face. There can be no question of an entanglement. She is to be kept at arm's length at all costs!*

Assuming as cool a demeanor as he could manage without seeming rude, he had decided to keep quiet about having seen her out riding earlier. In fact, he had thought it better not to engage her in conversation at all beyond basic civilities if he could help it.

Then, how to explain the sting he had felt at her look of utter panic when she greeted him so awkwardly?

How to explain his inability to think about anything else but her while he and Ralph waited for her to join them in the dining room. Though they kept up their usual cheerful banter, he could tell Ralph was worried she was not going to come at all.

It dawned on him that he was the cause of tension between the siblings. Lady Abby's cold reception had made it clear she objected to his presence at Worsley. *But how can she object to me when she doesn't even know me? Because she's a reclusive old maid who dislikes strangers, and I am a stranger who is moving into her home. According to Ralph, she also hates the Season and shuns the Ton. An oddity to say the least. Especially when she looks like an angel. She doesn't seem to be a lunatic either. So, why is she still single?*

And why is she so afraid of me?

A few minutes later, Ralph's eyes brightened, and Damian unconsciously held his breath as they heard the delicate tip-tap of light feet descending the stairs. An unaccountable thrill ran up Damian's spine. *She's coming!*

"Ah, here she is at last," Ralph said, smiling with obvious relief as both he and Damian looked expectantly at the door.

* * *

She's breathtaking in that quaintly demure blue gown, and I like the unusual way she has her hair cascading over one shoulder like that. Very original. And she's clearly no slave to fashion, which is admirable.

Damian caught himself admiring the way the flickering candlelight from the chandeliers above them danced across Lady Abby's hair as she sat directly opposite him at the dinner table.

With just the three of them, it was an intimate setting, and though he tried hard to maintain his cool façade throughout the meal, talking mainly to Ralph, he was nevertheless intensely aware of her presence the whole time, sneaking covert glances at her whenever he got the chance. He could not account for his disappointment when he did not catch her looking at him once.

In fact, she practically ignored him, radiating a frostiness that was almost tangible. While she ate almost nothing, the contents of her plate appeared to fascinate her. She only spoke when spoken to, her frequently monosyllabic responses to his and Ralph's attempts to draw her into the conversation giving the clear impression she did not want to be there.

Or rather, she does not want me to be here.

It was utterly ridiculous of him, he knew, to feel irked by it. Yet irked he was. *I should be grateful she dislikes me*, he told himself sternly, *and not simpering and hanging on my every word. It's a blessing indeed that she seems not to regard me as husband material.*

However, as time went on, he found her reticence so provoking, he could not resist the urge to try to make her talk to him.

"Ralph tells me you also have a passion for horses, Lady Abby. I should be very interested to hear what you think of our new business venture," he said, trying not to inject too much warmth into his voice, only the requisite polite interest.

"I support Ralph in whatever he does," she replied neutrally, her voice delightfully dulcet. "I wish for the venture to flourish for his sake, naturally."

Why will she not meet my eyes?

"Of course. Such loyalty to your brother is laudable. But I am certain that with your knowledge and experience of horseflesh, you will be able to offer some valuable insights to help make it a success."

"I am certain you have no need of my insights, Mr. Ross."

He was taken aback by the edge of bitterness in her tone. "Oh? May I ask why that is?"

"Ralph has told me of your expertise in the business. I cannot compete with that."

"There's no question of competing, Abby," Ralph put in. "Your opinions will always be welcome."

"I shall bear that in mind," she answered, flashing her brother a skeptical look with those remarkable silvery eyes of hers.

Damian was growing more confused by the minute. Part of him knew he should be happy about not having to fend off her advances, as previously feared. He would be able to focus on his work without distraction.

But that part was struggling against the powerful attraction Lady Abby exerted over him. Ralph had told him she disliked strangers, but this obvious rejection felt more personal. Absurd as it was, he had to admit, he found her inexplicable coldness hurtful.

He was unused to such treatment. As Viscount Amberley, heir to the Earl of Chartringham, he had grown used to single ladies fawning over him, actively pursuing him as the fox hunts the hare. He had bitterly complained of it many times. But right now ... he could not help thinking a little of that fawning from Lady Abby would not go amiss.

He found himself unfathomably disappointed when she suddenly rose from her seat just as pudding was coming round, saying, "I'm afraid you will have to excuse me. I have a megrim coming on and must retire directly. Good night."

With hardly a parting glance, she was gone. Damian looked at Ralph, hoping for an explanation of his sister's strange behavior. His host merely shrugged sheepishly and said, "Don't mind her, old chap. She's shy, but she'll be fine once she gets to know you."

Damian smiled and drank his wine to hide his consternation.

* * *

He was at the stables early the following morning, determined to learn his way about and make friends with the grooms. One of the lads, Billy, was off sick with a flu, and Damian had taken off his coat and was in his shirtsleeves, helping to muck out one of the stalls when Lady Abby strode in. For some unfathomable reason, he felt slightly embarrassed at her seeing him so disheveled.

But that was before he noticed her mode of dress. His jaw dropped, and he could not help staring at her. Her riding habit—today, a divine midnight blue that emphasized the autumnal tints of her hair—appeared at first perfectly normal. The superb tailoring fitted her admirable curves like a glove. But when she moved, he was astonished to see the flowing skirts were actually divided in two.

Realizing the implication, Damian felt a thrill course through him. The skirt was designed so she could ride astride! He would never forget the mesmerizing sight of her galloping astride at breakneck speed across the hills, bent low in the saddle, standing up in the stirrups. Just like man.

He silently marveled at her. She was shy, cold, refused to meet his eyes, and she hated his presence in her home. But she was also scandalous, rebellious, unafraid to fly in the face of history and convention by riding astride instead of sidesaddle as a lady ought. *What a woman!*

"Where is Billy today?" she asked, glancing around the interior for the missing groom. Her eyes widened as they alighted upon Damian. His soul shriveled a little at the way her smile abruptly vanished and the blood drained from her face. Once again, he spied fear in her eyes. And behind that, a sadness so deep it touched his heart and made him wonder at its cause.

"Good morning to you, Lady Abby," he said, keeping a tight rein on his composure.

A small, strained smile appeared on her face, but she did at least meet his eyes this time. However, hers were like chips of blue ice that bored into his.

"Good day to you, Mr. Ross," she replied in clipped tones, gently thwacking her gloved palm with her riding crop.

"You're an early bird indeed," he ventured.

"As are you," she said, dropping her gaze to the piles of straw-clogged dung surrounding him. "I see you have made yourself at home."

He ignored the sarcasm in her voice. "Billy is ill, apparently, so I'm just helping out where I can," he replied, feeling the chilly tension in the air rising.

"How laudable." Without another word, she turned smartly on her little heel and launched into a conversation with Quinton, the head groom.

"Is that right, Quinton? Billy has a flu?" she asked.

Quinton looked up mildly from the saddle he was polishing and nodded. "Aye, Milady, he's in a bad way, so his ma says."

"Oh, dear. Poor thing. He has such a weak chest. I shall send some medicine and some of Mrs. O'Connor's restorative broth over later, to help him mend. So, who shall ride out with me today? The horses must have their exercise," she added.

"Michael can go. He can take Silver and Ruby out for a stretch," Quinton said, gesturing with his chin to a lanky lad of about eighteen, who was assisting Damian with the mucking out. Michael grinned and immediately abandoned his pitchfork.

"Very well," Lady Abby replied decisively. "I shall take Warrior and Target."

Considering all the promises he had made to himself to remain aloof, Damian could not understand what compelled him to do what he did next.

As if from a distance, he heard himself say, "Lady Abby, I should like to come with you and Michael. I have not yet had the chance to see the estate, and it would be an ideal opportunity to get the lay of the land. It would also mean exercising six horses rather than four, which would be helpful since we're shorthanded. If you have no objection to my accompanying you, that is."

He added the last part hoping good manners would force her to agree.

She turned to him, a strange mixture of annoyance and fear on her face. As he had predicted, politeness won out, for she nodded. "If you wish. Quinton will tell you which of the horses to take out."

So, off they went, him, Lady Abby, and Michael, cantering across the fields and up the forested sides of the hills, each leading an extra horse behind them, to the gallops along the top. There, with the wind flying through his hair, Damian reveled in the exhilaration that racing along at speed on the back of a horse always brought with it.

It was the thing he liked to do best in all the world. However, that day, he discovered the thrill was greatly enhanced by thundering over the turf a few paces behind a beautiful girl riding daringly astride, who clearly took the same pleasure in the activity as himself.

He ignored the fact she did not speak a word to him the entire time they were out. Again, he told himself it was better that way, that he really did want to see the estate and was not tagging along simply because he was curious about her. And wanted to keep looking at her.

But on their return to the stables about an hour later, when she continued to ignore him and immediately took out another couple of horses, he found it bothered him. Moreover, he was bothered that it bothered him.

Chapter Four

"Really, Claire, it's awful. He's hardly been at Worsley for a day, and I'm already at my wit's end. My peace of mind is quite shattered," Abby was complaining bitterly to her best friend Claire Potter, the daughter of the local vicar, as they walked side by side along a quiet farm lane bordering the estate.

When she had ridden away from the stables earlier, desperate to relieve the pressure of being in Mr. Ross's company, Abby had galloped furiously across the fields and happened to spy Claire walking from the nearby cluster of farm cottages towards the village. With an urgent need to vent her woes to her friend, she had immediately turned her mare and made a beeline for her.

"Claire! Claire!" she had shouted in most unladylike manner, completely flustered by the morning's events so far. She saw Claire stop and wave at her from the lane. "Wait for me, will you, please? I have much to tell you," Abby called to her, geeing Tilly forward with her heels to quickly close the gap between them. Once in the lane, she had dismounted, and the friends shared warm greetings before Abby joined Claire on her walk home, leading Tilly behind her.

"You seem rather agitated, Abby," Claire observed at once, her sweet, round face crinkling with concern from beneath her bonnet. She peered at Abby through her spectacles. "Whatever is the matter?"

"Something dreadful," Abby had informed her, going on to describe the horrible surprise Ralph had sprung on her the day before.

"Oh, dear, that is dreadful indeed," Claire commiserated. "It beggars belief that your dear brother would do such a thing. But I suppose he feels it is necessary to have this Mr. Ross living at Worsley for the business' sake, does he?"

"So he says. He says I am good with horses but no good at dealing with people. And Mr. Ross is, apparently."

"Does he? That is extraordinarily blunt, but that is brothers for you. But well, dear, there is a little truth in that, is there not? You do hide away from people and prefer not to have visitors at Worsley," Claire pointed out.

"Yes, I do, but you know very well why that is, Claire. And so does Ralph, so he knows bringing Mr. Ross coming to live with us for goodness knows how long is like torture to me. And giving him the role I planned for myself is, well, it is like a slap in the face," Abby replied, deeply aggrieved.

"That is a little dramatic, Abby," said the ever-sensible Claire, whom Abby appreciated greatly for her calming abilities. "I know you must be very disappointed, but as Father is always saying, facts are facts. I presume one cannot successfully run a business if one dislikes meeting people. It would seem to be one of the prerequisites."

"I know that, you goose! I have already accepted that Mr. Ross is my superior in that respect. But do I not have the right to be angry that he has usurped both my role in the venture *and* my dream of training a Derby winner for my brother? You know how I had my heart set on being the one to do it for Ralph because he has been so good to me, and I give him so little in return."

"What silly nonsense, dear! Give so little? Why, no brother could hope to have a sister more concerned for his welfare or happiness than you are for Ralph's. And he adores you for it. You worry a little too much about him sometimes, I think."

"I cannot help but think he stays in the country so I won't be alone, when he would probably be much happier in London. Think of what he's missing out on because of me."

"I cannot speak about that, Abby, as I have never been to London and certainly have no experience of grand society. But I am sure Ralph stays at Worsley because he likes it. It is his home, after all. You really must stop feeling so bad about it."

"Hmm," Abby murmured noncommittally, sure she would never be able to do that.

"The fact that he and Mr. Ross plan to base the business at Worsley proves he prefers the country, does it not? That is a boon, surely? But one it seems you will have to balance against the unwelcome presence of Mr. Ross in your life. One could say it is a small sacrifice to make in order to make your brother happy. That way, you would not need to feel guilty at all. And did you not mention that at dinner last night, both Ralph and Mr. Ross said how they would value your opinions?"

Abby sighed. "Yes, I did mention that. But I do not believe Mr. Ross cares a jot for any of my opinions. He is already pushing his way in, getting his feet under the table. You know I am always at the stables just after seven. Well, when I walked in this morning, he was already there, helping the grooms to muck out if you please. I was so shocked, I could hardly think let alone speak. I hardly know how I did not simply run out."

"What a dreadful man! Helping to muck out, was he? How dare he take such liberties with your manure," Claire said, clearly stifling a small giggle behind her glove.

Abby blushed and failed to curb her smile. "I know you think me foolish, Claire, but I am seriously unnerved by all this sudden change. Having a stranger thrust upon me like this, it is hard for me. People have said such unkind things to me in the past about my disfigurement, I admit, I have hidden away, for I am fearful of fresh judgment. Yet having Mr. Ross at Worsley is an ordeal I cannot escape. You are afeared of snakes, are you not?"

Claire shuddered. "Horrid creatures!"

"Well, I feel the same way about strangers. In this case, Mr. Damian Ross."

They came to the crossroads at the corner of the churchyard and halted. "What sort of gentleman is he, Abby? Is he young? Old? Is he ill-mannered? Does he slurp his soup at dinner?"

Abby snorted with laughter despite herself. "I did not hear him slurping," she admitted, "and he appeared to have control of his silverware throughout. And, no, he has not been rude to me at all. In fact, he probably thinks me rude. I find myself quite overcome with nervousness in the company of strangers, as you know, and become tongue-tied. It was the same at dinner last night. I did not want to go at all, but Maude persuaded me I had to because she said otherwise I should have to eat my dinner alone in my chambers every night."

"Sensible lass," Claire remarked with an approving nod.

"But I am angry with Mr. Ross as well."

"For simply being there."

"Yes. For being at Worsley and ruining my plans. How can I not be? I resent him absolutely, and I do not apologize for it."

"Then I shall not counsel you to do so, dear, since you are so decided on the matter. After all, just because he is a lone gentleman in a strange place, why should he be in need of the hand of friendship?"

"Oh, Claire, how dare you try to make me feel sorry for him!"

"If the cap fits, Abby dear, then one might as well wear it."

"I do not wear a cap," Abby countered, and they both laughed. "You are making me feel better, my dear friend, even though you are being quite horrid in the things you say." She hesitated for a moment, unsure of how to word what she sought to express to her friend. "It is not just that I am finding Mr. Ross's presence at Worsley an imposition because he is a stranger to me, Claire. He is ... he is ... he makes me feel ... odd."

"Odd? In what way odd?" Claire scrutinized her closely, her melting brown eyes through the lenses of her eyeglasses full of curiosity. Abby guessed there must be something in her expression that told Claire exactly why Mr. Ross made her feel odd, because her friend's lips suddenly curved upward into a huge smile.

"Are you trying to say he is handsome, Abby?" she asked teasingly, her eyes sparkling with mischief.

Abby felt her cheeks flare. "I suppose you could describe him as reasonably pleasant to look upon," she admitted grudgingly.

"Oh! So, he is *very* handsome then. And is he young too?"

"He was in the same year as Ralph at Eton, so they are the same age."

"Not quite thirty then, and devilishly handsome. I see. And is there a Mrs. Ross by any chance?"

Abby was shocked that she had not even thought of such a possibility. And now she did, she found it vexing that, for some unknown reason, part of her strongly objected to the notion of a Mrs. Ross. Not just on the grounds that she would be yet another stranger to deal with either. But she did not say that to Claire because she did not even want to admit it to herself.

"Oh, I do not know. I did not ask. There may be, I suppose. But if she exists, she has not been mentioned. Nor have any children. Would he come and live with us if he had a wife, do you think?"

Claire shrugged. "It seems unlikely, but perhaps you should make sure just in case."

"In case of what?" Abby inquired innocently.

"Why, in case you should fall in love with him, of course! Or he with you."

Abby gasped, genuinely shocked, while Claire laughed. "I am teasing you, of course. Such a thing will never happen. You could never fall for such a monstrous fellow as Mr. Damian Ross, I am sure."

Abby laughed nervously, unsettled by her friend's playful words. For a moment, she let herself imagine she was in a crowded ballroom, dressed in all her finery, and she met those startlingly green eyes through a break in the crowd.

Her heart skipped a beat just to think of what the possibilities for happiness might have been. *If not for the fire.*

"Abby? Abby? A penny for your thoughts." Claire's voice called her back to reality.

"Sorry, forgive me, I was miles away for a moment," she confessed.

"Oh, you suddenly look so sad, dear. Do not mind my jesting. I should hate to think my silly prattle has upset you," Claire said contritely.

"No, no, you could never upset me. It is just that talk of love and romance, well, it always reminds me of what I have lost. You know I have given up all hope of ever marrying and having a family of my own because of what happened to me. The *Ton* is right. No gentleman will ever wish to wed a disfigured lady like me. Not one to whom I would wish to be wed at any rate. As you know, I am quite resigned to being an old maid."

"Well, if Mr. Fielding does not hurry up and propose to me soon, then we shall be old maids together," Claire replied, clearly trying to lighten Abby's sad mood. Mr. Fielding was the church sexton, and he and Claire had been courting for two years. She was waiting on tenterhooks for him to propose any day, and it had become rather a game for the two girls to wager if he would finally say the words whenever he called on Claire.

Appreciating Claire's attempt to cheer her, she laughed with her friend, and her sad mood lifted a little. Claire's company always calmed her frazzled mind and allowed her to read her thoughts and feelings more clearly.

It prompted her to say, "I suppose I could get used to Mr. Ross being about the place, as long as he is not always under my feet at the stables or in the house. And he does not interfere with my horses."

"That is very Christian of you, dear. Father would approve," Claire replied with a smile, opening the churchyard gate so they could walk along the path around the church leading to the vicarage.

"But I suppose I am frightened that if I let my guard down and allow myself to be friends with him, then it would be ten times more painful if he found out about my disfigurement and was repulsed." She had not realized it before, but now that his presence was a *fait accompli*, she could see it was her foremost fear. "Which he is bound to be."

"Not necessarily, Abby. You fear judgment, but are you not judging him now, without even knowing him?"

"Yes, I suppose so. But no, Claire, I do not think I can take the risk. I cannot be his friend, even if it makes me a bad person. It is better to keep my distance. That way, I cannot be hurt again."

Chapter Five

"What d'you say we go for a ride? It's a lovely day, and I'm fed up being cooped up indoors," Ralph said, yawning widely as he rose from his study chair and stretched his arms above his head. " Besides, even though you saw a bit of it yesterday with Abby, you still need a proper tour of the estate."

"I like the sound of that," Damian agreed, getting to his feet as well, glad to exchange the documents and plans covering Ralph's desk for some fresh air. They had spent a couple of hours since luncheon absorbed in their preparations, and he was starting to feel sleepy.

They left the study and went upstairs, agreeing to change and then meet at the stables as soon as they were ready.

Within the hour, Damian found himself mounted on Silver, a two-year-old thoroughbred colt, cantering across the sunny open fields and low wooded hills of the Lucas estate. At his side, laughing heartily as they flew along, was Ralph, astride his favorite Arab stallion, five-year-old Warrior. Ralph wanted Damian's opinion on the form of the two potential race winners, which were destined to form the basis of the new business's breeding program.

They were thundering along when disaster suddenly struck, in the form of a panicked cock pheasant. In a flurry of brightly colored feathers, it burst from its hiding place behind some tufted weeds, spooking Warrior in the process. The stallion baulked and reared violently, throwing a helpless Ralph from the saddle, sending him crashing to the turf below.

Terrified for his friend, Damian reined Silver in sharply and dismounted. He ran over to the now groaning Ralph, hoping the grass had provided him with a relatively soft landing and no serious injuries. Thankfully, Ralph was already sitting up when he reached him, but grimacing with pain.

Damian squatted at his side. "Bad luck, old man, but at least you're alive. Good job you took a tumble on grass, eh? Anything broken?" he asked with concern.

"I'm afraid so, blast that pheasant!" Ralph replied in an aggrieved tone. "I think I've gone and broken my leg."

That was the last thing he uttered before passing out, which was when Damian noticed the large lump on the side of his head. Knowing the potential danger of such injuries, he wasted no time in going to fetch help.

* * *

"But Sir Henry has already been sent for, Milady. And the bonesetter as well," Damian heard Withers inform Lady Abby after she issued those same instructions to him. He had been standing by the bed when she came rushing into Ralph's chambers. His heart went out to her when she stopped in her tracks, seeing terror in her eyes.

"Is he ... is he ...?" she had asked hesitantly in a small voice, unexpectedly looking to him for an answer.

Wanting to reassure her, he had quickly shaken his head. "No, he's just fainted, that's all. It's the pain from his leg, I expect."

"Oh, thank the Lord," she breathed, bustling to the other side of the bed and taking Ralph's limp hand in hers. "Withers, send for Sir Henry and the bonesetter immediately. Hurry, please," she instructed the hovering butler.

Withers explained things to her. And that was when the trouble started.

"Pardon? How can that be so when I have only just been informed of what has happened?" she asked, shooting the butler a puzzled look.

Seeing Wither's discomfiture, Damian stepped in. "Forgive me, Lady Abby, but I gave the order to summon the physician and the bonesetter myself as soon as Ralph was brought home. I did not know where you were, and, in the circumstances, I deemed it of the utmost urgency to do so."

"I see," she replied, giving him a tight-lipped little glance before resuming her worried examination of the unconscious Ralph. "Well, I was only in my chambers and came directly. But I thank you for so promptly taking control of the situation, Mr. Ross."

Despite her words of gratitude, Damian sensed displeasure in her rather waspish tone and was confused by it. *Surely, she cannot be annoyed with me for giving the orders, can she?* Though it seemed a ridiculous possibility, he nevertheless felt pressured to justify himself.

"Your brother has taken a nasty knock to his head, Lady Abby. Such injuries can be dangerous if not seen to as soon as possible. He has also broken his leg."

"Yes, I can see that, thank you." She turned and ordered one of the maids hovering nearby to bring cold water and cloths, just as another entered the drawing room carrying exactly those items.

"I also took the liberty of ordering, er, those," Damian put in, gesturing with his eyes at the things as the maid set them on the nightstand.

"Then I have further cause to thank you," Lady Abby muttered tightly, perching on the edge of the bed and commencing to lay damp, cooling cloths over the lump on Ralph's head, which was now dark-blue and the size of a hen's egg.

Putting her odd behavior down to shock and worry, Damian strode over to Withers and said quietly, "You may go now, Withers, but send up some tea and bring the physician in as soon as he arrives, please." He had another thought. "Oh, you had better leave the door open while we wait for him, I suppose," he added, mindful of Lady Abby's reputation.

The butler understood at once—they should not be left alone in the room with the door closed, with no one but an unconscious man as chaperone. Withers complied with a nod and silently glided from the room, leaving the door wide open.

"Withers, you may go about your duties," Lady Abby suddenly said, glancing over her shoulder. "I shall ring if I ... Oh, he has gone," she added with a puzzled frown.

"I dismissed him, Lady Abby. It's best for Ralph to rest quietly while we wait for the physician," Damian told her.

"I see you have once again taken charge of the situation on my behalf," she replied without looking at him, placing an icy emphasis on "taken charge of the situation," which left him in no doubt she was annoyed with him. Against his better judgment, Damian once more felt driven to defend himself.

"I fear I have offended you, Lady Abby. If so, I apologize for it. But as to the rest, I cannot be sorry. You mention my taking charge of the situation as if it were a bad thing. I ask you to reconsider. Time was of the essence, and I acted purely out of concern for Ralph's wellbeing. As his sister, I did not foresee you taking a different view."

He had said much more, and far more candidly, than intended. But his sense of injustice had been roused, and the words had just kept coming. Also, tiresome though it was to admit, he had the absurd desire for her to think well of him.

She finally met his eyes across the bed, and he was struck by the way her eyes flashed with controlled fury. It was strangely exciting. *By George,* he thought, *she's even more ravishing when she's angry!*

"Are you trying to imply that I do not care about my brother's wellbeing?" she demanded in a dangerously calm voice, looking as though she would like to set about him with her fists.

"Of course not! I'm simply politely expressing my puzzlement as to why you seem so angry with me. Clearly, you feel I have usurped your authority in some way, but is not taking charge what ladies generally like gentlemen to do in such situations?"

"I do not know what you are talking about, sir."

"Then, pray, explain to me why you appear so annoyed with me."

"Annoyed with you, Mr. Ross?" She gave a tinkling laugh of polite derision that rang false to his ears. "You are mistaken. I assure you, I harbor no such strong emotion concerning you. If I seem a little exercised, it is merely out of anxiety for my brother."

"For the Lord's sake, you two, will you stop bickering?" came an aggrieved croak from the bed. "My head is splitting already, and you're just making it worse."

The bickering stopped long enough for both Damian and Lady Abby to express their relief that Ralph was awake and seemed in his right mind. Though, clearly, he was in a lot of pain from his broken leg. However, when Sir Henry arrived a short while later, hostilities surfaced again.

"I can manage from here, thank you, Mr. Ross," Lady Abby told Damian pertly while Sir Henry was checking Ralph's vital signs. "There is really no need for you to trouble yourself further. I am sure you have other things to do."

"But I wish to remain, Lady Abby. Ralph is my friend. I was with him when he fell, and I want to hear what the physician has to say about his injuries," he protested mildly, wondering what she was about.

"I'm sure Ralph will be able to tell you that himself after the examination. I am his sister and, therefore, closest to him. Obviously, I must remain, whereas your presence is unnecessary and may prove distracting for Sir Henry."

Lord, she is vexing!

"You speak in jest, of course, Lady Abby, for we both know I could hardly distract Sir Henry by simply standing here. What do you say, Sir Henry?"

The aged physician's bushy eyebrows beetled disapprovingly as he looked from one to the other as though at naughty children. "It would be best for His Lordship if I examined him alone," he answered with gruff impatience.

This is her fault, Damian thought irritably, *for trying to make me leave when there's no good reason for it. Except her dislike of me. It serves her right that if I have to go, then so does she!*

"Hear, hear, Sir Henry. I heartily thank you for voicing my very own thoughts," Ralph said querulously. "Would you please both wait outside? You really are making my headache worse."

"I apologize, my friend. Sir Henry, forgive me," Damian said with a contrite nod, immediately heading for the door, glad she would have to follow him.

But she hesitated and was clearly about to protest when Ralph said sternly, "Out at once if you please, Sister."

"Oh, very well," she huffed, looking daggers at Damian as he held the door open for her and she passed into the hall before him. Although he was annoyed with himself for being drawn into conflict with her, he could not stop himself from glaring right back.

The instant he shut the door, she wheeled on him.

"Mr. Ross, I hold you wholly responsible for my being banished from Ralph's side like this when he needs me most," she berated him.

Unaccountably stung by the injustice of her claim, Damian defended himself. "Lady Abby, allow me to point out that if you had not so relentlessly insisted I leave, for no good reason, I might add, then neither of us would be standing out here now."

She scoffed. "For no good reason?! I beg to differ. I am family. You are not. Yet you have somehow contrived to have me dismissed as well."

"I have already explained my reasons for wishing to stay with my friend and fail to see why you should object to it," Damian retorted. Then, lowering his voice, he added meaningfully, "Unless there is some hidden reason for it of which I am unaware."

She went off like a little firework, eyes blazing, hands on hips. "As a matter of fact, there is."

Chapter Six

"Oh?" Damian replied with feigned casualness, not having bargained on such forthrightness. "Please, do not hold back. I am genuinely interested to hear what you have to say," he added, dying to know what she had against him.

"You are not welcome here. I do not want you here. I wish you would leave and that we should never meet again," she said with unexpected venom.

Concealing how taken aback he was by her brutal admission, he replied cooly, "I appreciate your frankness, but you have me at a disadvantage. You still have not explained your reasons for taking against me so vehemently."

She took a step towards him. "You speak of the business venture in which you and Ralph are now partners. Did you know it was originally my idea?"

He was surprised. "I admit I did not. Is it relevant?"

"It most certainly is. *I* planned to be my brother's business partner. *I* wanted to be the one to train his Derby winner. By coming here, you have ruined my most cherished dream!"

Damian was so astonished, he could no longer disguise it, and felt himself faltering as her words sank in. *Lord, no wonder she hates me! I would hate me too if I were in her position.*

But then something occurred to him. "If that is the case, then I am sorry for it," he replied, meaning every word. "But Ralph must have his reasons for going into partnership with me instead of you. He has not discussed them with me, so I am ignorant in that respect. If you are aware of them, then perhaps you would enlighten me."

She did not answer but merely stood before him, her chest rising and falling rapidly, a spitfire with scarlet cheeks, flashing eyes, and small, clenched fists.

Despite the heated nature of their exchange, Damian's heart beat a little faster just looking at her. He waited on tenterhooks for her answer, watching curiously as a storm of indecision raged in her eyes. But it seemed that every time she was on the verge of saying something, she thought better of it and bit back her tongue.

So, they simply stared at each other for several moments in fraught silence. Until the sound of the chamber door opening broke the spell, and they turned in unison to see Sir Henry standing on the threshold.

"I have completed my examination of His Lordship, and he says you may come in now," he told them.

* * *

Abby was still trembling from the unfinished confrontation with Damian as they entered Ralph's bedroom. In truth, it had upset her so much, she had all but forgotten poor Ralph's plight. So, when she saw his pale, drawn face as he stretched out on the bed, she felt a pang of guilt. Although he was manfully doing his best to hide it, it was obvious his leg was very painful.

"How is he, Sir Henry? He will make a full recovery, will he not?" she asked anxiously, hurrying to her brother's side.

"I see no reason why not," the physician said, packing up his bag. "But he has taken a nasty knock to the head, and it remains to be seen if it has caused a concussion. You must watch him very carefully for any signs of confusion or sickness for at least the next twenty-four hours. Keep him awake as long as possible. And when he does sleep, wake him at regular intervals to check on him."

Relief swept over her. "Of course, I will make sure of it. Thank you, Sir Henry." She smiled down at Ralph, but he scowled back at her.

"It might knock some brains into me, I suppose," he grumbled. "Lord, what bad luck. What a fool I am!"

"I have given him something for the pain from the leg," the physician continued, indicating with a nod a small medicine bottle on a side table. "Give him two teaspoonfuls of that when he needs it, but no more. I can do nothing for his leg. The bonesetter must see to that. I shall call again in the morning. I bid you good day."

She was surprised when Damian volunteered to see Sir Henry out. While he was gone, she took Ralph's hand and squeezed it.

"Well, this is a rum do," he muttered with bitter disappointment. "I never bargained on being stuck with a broken leg. Six weeks it will take to mend at the very least. Six weeks of being stuck in bed, able to do precisely nothing."

"I'm so sorry, Ralph, I know it must be awful for you. But the main thing is that you are alive and will, in time, be perfectly well again," she told him, full of sympathy. "Apart from the possible concussion that is. But I shall stay up with you all night if necessary and keep you entertained."

"So shall I, my dear friend." She jumped as the now familiar deep voice came from behind her. Damian was back, and he was standing right next to her. An uncomfortable heat prickled her skin at his close proximity, and she was about to move away on the pretext of ringing for some tea when a maid appeared in the doorway carrying a fully laden tea tray.

Why must the wretched man preempt me at every turn? Abby thought pettishly as she directed the girl to set it down on the console table. *It is as though he can read my mind and does it just to annoy me.* Nevertheless, she was grateful for the distraction the tea provided.

Damian commiserated with Ralph whilst she wielded the teapot, so she took the opportunity to reflect on their clash. She had never meant to go so far as to tell him about how he had ruined her plans and bitterly regretted losing her temper in front of him. Rationally, she knew she was being unfair to him. *Ralph invited him to Worsley. He is the best person for the job. None of it is his fault.*

Yet it seemed that whenever he was anywhere near her, her capacity to think straight flew out of the window. In his presence, she trembled, she blushed like schoolgirl, and her heart was constantly at war with her head. She hated the feeling of being out of control. Besides that, she cringed inwardly to know she had embarrassed herself yet again and must seem even more foolish in his eyes.

* * *

A short while later, the bonesetter and his assistant arrived to set Ralph's leg, and she and Damian were once more banished from the room, but for much longer this time. The bonesetter said it was a compound fracture that would take at least an hour to set.

Out in the hall, she was expecting Damian to pick up their earlier argument. In fact, perverse though she knew it was, she was secretly looking forward to sparring with him again. But he said nothing.

Instead, he merely inclined his head to her before striding away to the rear of the house, heading for the stables, she assumed.

Feeling strangely disappointed, she retreated to the library, where she tried to read a book. But troublesome thoughts of Damian vied with Ralph's faint cries of agony, which floated down the stairs. Her eyes scanned the same paragraph over and over again, taking in nothing of its meaning at all.

Later, once the bonesetter had done his work and departed, she arranged for dinner to be served in Ralph's chambers, to keep him company and make sure he stayed awake as long as possible that day, as Sir Henry had instructed.

The huge weight of the splints and stiffened bandages that would keep his leg in place for the next six weeks meant he would be confined to his bed for the duration. Of course, it was inevitable that Damian would join them there for dinner.

After their earlier disagreement, Abby was even more aware of the tension cracking between the two of them as they dined in unusually informal circumstances. The air in Ralph's chamber felt heavy with words unsaid, ratcheting up her nerves and robbing her of appetite. She pushed morsels of rabbit pie, one of her favorites, around her plate, eating little.

She listened in silence while Damian and Ralph kept up a constant stream of talk about business and mutual acquaintances and such like as they tucked into Mrs. O'Connor's excellent rabbit pie with apparent gusto. She could not explain to herself why she should feel put out that they no longer bothered to try to draw her into the conversation when she knew it was her own fault. Yet she did.

Ralph seemed oblivious to the tension between them, but Abby knew he was far from it. In fact, he likely held her responsible for it because he had told her so in private. Her mind went back to the difficult exchange they had shared a few days before when he had caught her alone in the library.

"I know it's hard for you, Abby, but perhaps you could try to be a little more friendly towards Damian, especially during dinner. Don't think I haven't noticed you giving him the cold shoulder," he had begun, his tone mild.

"That is not true!" she had exclaimed, snapping her book shut, bristling at the home truth.

Ralph had sighed and stuck his hands in his pockets. "I'm not blind, Abby. You've hardly spoken a word to the poor fellow since he arrived."

"You know I do not like strangers," she had tried to argue again, her insides squirming with discomfort. She hated it when Ralph was unhappy with her. "It takes time for me to get used to people."

"But he's been here a week, so he's hardly a stranger now, is he?"

"Maybe not to you, but he will always be a stranger to me," she had replied, knowing she was being unreasonable but quite unable to give way.

How could she explain to Ralph the dangers that lay in dropping her guard? If she gave way to the attraction drawing her to Damian, and even if he liked her in return, as soon as he found out about her disfigurement, then rejection and heartache would surely follow.

She would never be able to face him again. He would probably leave Worsley out of sheer embarrassment, and then she would be responsible for ruining Ralph's dreams for the business. She could not live with that, not after all he had done for her.

So, what am I to do? I am in an impossible position. Oh, it's all such a muddle, I cannot think straight! she had thought in a panic.

"Look, Abby, Damian's going to be living with us for the foreseeable future. He's a jolly good fellow and a trusted friend and business partner. Do me a favor and try having an actual conversation with him, get to know him. There's only so long I can make excuses for you."

That hurt a lot. "I suppose he's complained about me, has he?" she asked, suspicion flaring.

"Don't be any more of a goose than you already are, Abby," Ralph had told her kindly. "Damian is a gentleman and far above such sneaking behavior. No, this is me telling you that I'd appreciate your cooperation in this. For my sake, will you at least try?"

"I'll think about it," she had replied through gritted teeth before shutting the door on him.

Apart from Ralph's recovery, she had thought of little else since. And knowing she was displeasing Ralph by appearing to resist what seemed to him a reasonable request was making the storm of guilt and confusion already raging inside her even worse.

Somehow, I am going to have to find a balance between keeping Damian at a distance and showing Ralph that I'm trying to do as he wishes. But how?

She had hardly any chance to think about it further because as soon as dinner was over, Ralph dropped a bombshell that sent her into fresh turmoil.

"Obviously, I shan't be able to attend the horse fair with you as planned, Damian, old chap," he suddenly said casually. "So, I thought it would be good if Abby went with you instead. She's a better judge of horseflesh than I am anyway. I'm sure that together, you'll do very well in selecting a couple of good bets. That all right with you?"

Abby was stunned and reflexively looked at Damian. She thought she saw a moment of panic in his eyes that reflected her own. It gave her pause. *Is he as uncomfortable about going with me as I am with him?* she wondered, unexpectedly hurt by the idea, even though it showed her defenses were working.

But if it were panic, it soon vanished, and so she told herself she had imagined it.

"Of course, what a delightful idea," Damian replied with an affable smile that gave nothing of his real thoughts away. He shot her an inscrutable glance that made her quiver. "Lady Abby's knowledge and experience of horses will be invaluable, I have no doubt."

Oh, Lord! I simply cannot go with him. How shall I get out of it? Abby wondered, her panic rising. Several possible excuses rushed through her head. But in the end, she knew it was no good.

If I do not go, then I shall be letting Ralph down, so I have no choice. I shall have to spend an entire day, out in public, with Damian. Oh, what a disaster!

Chapter Seven

Damian was still shaken by the earlier acrimonious exchange with Abby when Ralph made his shock announcement that she was to accompany him to the horse fair. Of course, he hid his concern at the prospect of spending so much time with her alone. But frankly, the whole idea scared him.

Abby's predictably horrified expression at Ralph's edict was unsurprising, yet it rankled. He watched her face and guessed she was desperately trying to think of an excuse why she could not go. But he also knew she would do nothing to disappoint her brother. Like him, she had no choice but to agree.

They would have to spend the whole day together, working together to select the right horses to buy. He doubted she would cooperate with him when selecting the horses. It could turn out to be very unpleasant.

Suddenly, something he had been looking forward to with unbridled enthusiasm took on an altogether more daunting dimension, and it filled him with nervous apprehension. *Oh, Lord! How will I survive it for a whole day without Ralph there to ease the tension?*

After several hands of whist, Ralph grew tired and needed his medicine, so Damian left the siblings and headed off to bed.

* * *

The next morning, after a fitful night in which a stern-faced Abby troubled his dreams, he rose early. Still weary, he fortified himself with strong coffee and a bite to eat, then went straight to the stables.

He tried to keep busy, taking two of the horses out for exercise, hoping the ride in the pleasant morning air would clear his head. It did no such thing. However hard he tried to enjoy the ride or focus on business plans, his thoughts always returned to the problem of Abby.

Though he was loath to admit it even to himself, he could no longer ignore the way the cold, resentful, utterly entrancing Abby was starting to occupy almost all of his thoughts. Even before their clash and Ralph's shock announcement about the horse fair, his feelings towards her had started to trouble him more than he was comfortable with.

What was truly worrying was that no matter how many times he reminded himself that he had sworn off romance and anything to do with matrimony for life, it made no difference. The attraction he felt for her was just too powerful to resist. Whenever they were in the same room, the tension was almost unbearable. It was doubly frustrating since she consistently gave him the cold shoulder, leaving him no chance whatsoever to try to win her over.

At night, he was having trouble sleeping because every time he closed his eyes, her face appeared in his mind and would not budge. He was not even safe when he was dreaming now, either, it seemed.

The truth was, he had never felt like this about a woman before, and it was by far the most terrifying thing that had ever happened to him.

Moreover, he could not seem to do anything to stop it. Abby Lucas drew him like the proverbial magnet. And the colder she was towards him, the more he felt compelled to rise to the challenge she presented, to break down her defenses and make her warm to him.

To think when I first came here, I was worried about being pursued by an old maid, he thought bitterly as he ran the curry comb across the horse's glossy flanks. *What a cruel joke! If I'm not careful, I'll turn into one of those love-sick fools I've always despised. Lord, I'll be writing poetry to her before long or serenading her beneath her bedroom window!*

I need advice and guidance, someone to keep me on the straight and narrow. I need to make good choices. But I can hardly talk to Ralph about it. What would I say? Your beautiful ice princess of a sister is driving me slowly insane? No. I need to talk to Lyle. But Lyle is in London, and there's absolutely no chance of getting him to come this far out of London.

An idea suddenly came to him. *I know. If I survive the horse fair, I'll take a few days off and go up and see him. Perhaps a little distance will help me to see things more clearly anyway. Yes, that's what I'll do.*

Until then, I'll continue to play it cool. Not let her have the satisfaction of knowing she's gotten under my skin. Keep things strictly business.

Having resolved on a course of action, he felt slightly happier and was able to enjoy the rest of his ride. However, when he got back to the stables, he was surprised to learn Abby had not yet arrived for her morning ride. That was very unusual, and he wondered if something was wrong to keep her away from her beloved horses. *Most likely, she's trying to avoid me. Well, that suits me just fine*, he told himself grimly.

But then it occurred to him it could be something to do with Ralph and his concussion, and he suddenly recalled that Sir Henry had promised to call back that morning to check on his friend. Concerned for his friend, he decided to go up to the house and find out.

He had just reached the closed door of Ralph's chamber when he heard the sound of raised voices coming from inside and stopped dead. In fact, there was only one raised voice, and it was unmistakably Abby's. Ralph was responding in the same calm, reasonable tone as always.

Damian knew he should leave, but the temptation to hear what she was so excited about was too overwhelming. So, he found himself frozen to the spot, shamefully eavesdropping like a nosy servant.

That shame was nothing to the horror he felt when a few moments later, before he had even had a chance to hear anything being said, the door suddenly flew open and Abby rushed out. There was no time to avoid her, and they collided.

"I'm sorry," he muttered in confusion, instinctively grabbing hold of her to steady her.

She dashed his hands away furiously. "You!" she hissed, staring at him with flashing eyes before turning on her heel and hurrying away to her chambers farther down the hall.

Dazed by the encounter, he watched her disappear into her room and winced as the door slammed loudly behind her. *What on earth is the matter with her?*

"Is that you, Damian, old chap?" Ralph's voice floated out to him. "Come in here and have some luncheon with me, will you? I could use some cheery company."

"Lady Abby seems upset," he ventured, entering Ralph's bedroom and seeing him propped up on his pillows, drinking coffee, with a large tray of food resting on the coverlet next to him.

"Yes, I believe she is a bit," Ralph replied, to Damian's amazement, apparently unconcerned by the scene that had just occurred. He gestured to the tray. "Come, sit down and partake of this feast. I'll never get through all this by myself. Mrs. O'Connor thinks a broken leg needs feeding, it seems."

Damian took the chair next to the bed. It was still pleasantly warm from where Abby had been sitting in it, which gave him an odd little thrill.

"Are you not worried about your sister?" he asked, helping himself to a cup of coffee.

Ralph laughed and gave him a pitying look. "You don't have any sisters, do you?"

"You know very well I don't," Damian replied, selecting a large sugared bun from the tray. "I am an only child."

"Well, my dear fellow, you have no idea how lucky you are."

* * *

Abby was galloping furiously across the meadows, urging Silver onward with her heels, trying to blow away the anger gripping her following the argument with Ralph—and the hideous embarrassment of rushing from the room in a temper and running straight into the last person she wanted to see at that moment, Damian Ross!

How long was he out there? she wondered as they flew across the turf. *How much of the argument did he hear?* She replayed the row in her mind, trying to remember what she had said about him that he might have overheard.

"Ralph, I'm begging you, please, do not make me go to the horse fair. You know I hate to have to mix with people in public like that. It will make me ill."

"I sympathize, Abby, and you know I wouldn't ask you to go if I had any choice in the matter. But you must realize that with my leg all plastered up like this, I need you to go instead of me."

"But it will be full of strangers! You know I cannot bear to be among people I do not know and trust. Truly, I shall be ill. I shall faint or something equally embarrassing, and that will make it even worse. Everyone will stare at me. Oh, do not make me go! Send Quinton instead."

"Quinton is a fine fellow, but I'd be mad to trust him with selecting the two most important assets to our fledgling business. I'm sorry, old girl, but it has to be you. Besides, you won't be on your own. Damian will be there to look after you."

She had scrunched up her fists at that and barely stifled the scream that threatened to burst out. As it was, she could hear her own voice rising in line with the agitation filling her.

"But can you not see, that is just going to make things even worse? He is a stranger, I do not know him, and I certainly do not trust him to "look after" me, as you put it. Being among all those people will be bad enough, but with him there to see me make a fool of myself, which is bound to happen, well, I would rather die."

"Come now, Sister, you exaggerate. Have more confidence in yourself. You are a very good judge of horseflesh. You and Damian are the only two people I trust to do the job properly. You shan't even have to talk to anyone if you don't want to. He'll handle all that. You are simply there to help him select the most promising horses, that is all."

"I cannot do it, I tell you! I cannot spend the entire day with that man!" she heard herself shouting, growing more and more fearful and frustrated with his refusal to see her point of view by the moment.

"Yes, you can. If you want to help make a go of the business, you'll do it, all right. Besides, you'll no doubt learn many useful things from Damian about establishing and running the venture. That will be very handy in the future." He looked at her with enraging calmness.

"No, no, no!"

"Yes, yes, yes. Abby, it is hard to say this to you, but I worry about you. You live buried here in the country like this, shutting yourself away from the world. That is not right, and it troubles me greatly to see my beloved sister rotting away. Do you not think I'm concerned about your future? I cannot believe that one as spirited as you can just give up on life and any hope of happiness, to die as a lonely old maid. I don't want that for you."

"I shall not be lonely. I have you," she protested, his words like knives in her heart.

He sighed. "You cannot rely on me being around forever. At any rate, have you ever thought that I might take a wife and have a family?"

Her heart squeezed painfully. "Yes. Yes, of course, I have."

"If that happened, then my wife would take over the running of the house. You would be displaced, and you would not like that."

"How could you, Ralph? Why are you being so cruel?!" she wailed in distress. He had never said things like this to her before, and the thought of losing her place as lady of the house to another stranger was agonizing. A strange woman who might see her as a financial burden.

A chilling vision flashed into her mind, of herself in ten years' time, a real old maid in black crêpe, likely relegated to a dusty garret by a wicked sister-in-law, a figure of fun to her nephews and nieces.

"If I am being cruel, then it is only because I care about you," he told her, her appeals sliding off him like water off a duck's back. "Abby, you're young, you should be out enjoying life while you can. You must make some effort to get over your fears and rejoin the human race. If you want to make me happy, then you must at least try. The horse fair is a good place to start. No more arguments. It's imperative that you do this thing for me. For all of us."

"Oh, I never thought it would come to this between us, Ralph!" she cried in anguish, his frightening words ringing in her mind like the

tolling of funeral bells. "You have made it so that I have no choice but to do as you ask. But do not blame me if it all goes wrong!"

Picking up her skirts, she ran out of the door . . .

Oh, Lord, what if Damian heard all that?! she thought, slowing the horse to a trot as a wave of nausea washed over her. She was not worried about Damian feeling insulted by her refusal to go with him. Had she not already told him why she resented him so much?

No, what was really worrying her was the thought that if he had heard it all, then he would know her greatest weakness, her fear of strangers, of being out in public. It felt like she had handed him a weapon to use against her.

Feeling queasy with anxiety, craving privacy and peace, to try to untangle the confusion raging in her head, she headed for the place that aways calmed her. Pulling up the reins, she dismounted. Leading Silver, she slowly walked them back across the meadows and down to the lake.

There, she let the horse drink while she took in the tranquil scene, seeking calm in the warmth of the air, the shimmering water, the gently swaying reeds that buzzed with bird and insect life, and the calls from the various waterfowl.

She walked out over the series of large stepping stones that reached out into the lake, which she and Ralph had so often played upon as children. She reached the last stone, feeling sure of her footing and with no fear of the water, even though it was at its deepest there and she had never quite mastered swimming, despite the amount of time they had spent on or near the water.

For a while, she stood there, watching the dragonflies dancing, letting her mind empty.

The duck burst from somewhere beneath her, a violently flapping, squawking, airborne ball of feathery protest that launched itself upwards in front of her and knocked her off balance.

"No, no, I am not going to ... Ah!" she cried, arms whirring as she struggled to save herself. But things had gone too far. With a hopeless feeling of dread, she felt herself fall with a loud splash into the cold lake water.

The air left her lungs as she plunged below the surface. Panicking when she could not feel ground beneath her feet, she inhaled a mouthful of water. She rose to the surface but only had time to snatch a quick breath before she went under again, dragged down by her heavy skirts.

This is it, I'm going to drown!

Bobbing to the surface again, praying someone would hear, she screamed for help as loudly as she could, feeling the urge to live surprisingly strong within her.

Chapter Eight

"Oh, Lord, it's Lady Abby!" Damian exclaimed, his heart lurching with fear when he identified the person thrashing frantically in the water and shouting for help.

He dropped his coat and sprinted as fast as he could down to the lake, pulling off his boots as he ran. Without a second thought, he ran straight into the bracingly cold shallows, switching to a fast crawl as the water deepened.

I have to save her! I have to!

"Help, help!" she cried, thrashing desperately before she went under again and then bobbed up, grappling uselessly at the air, gasping for breath.

"I'm coming, try not to panic!" he shouted to her, cleaving through the water as best he could in his trousers, vest, and shirt. When he finally reached her, she was in such a frenzy of fear, it took all his strength to calm her enough to allow him to tow her back to the shallows.

Once they reached them, seeing she was exhausted, terrified, and weighed down by her soaking skirts, Damian simply picked her up and carried her to the bank, laying her down carefully on the grass.

"You're safe now," he said reassuringly, kneeling beside her as she continued to pull breath into her lungs and cough up lake water. "Are you hurt?"

Despite her distress, she managed to give him a withering look that, for some reason, made him chuckle. It earned him an angry glare, which made him laugh out loud. He could not help but find it funny that he had just snatched her from the jaws of death, and rather than be grateful, she was so contrary as to be annoyed with him for it. *Stubborn as a mule and utterly unreasonable!*

Moreover, with her hair plastered to her head and her wet clothes clinging to her, she was a pitiful yet strangely appealing sight. Feeling the urge to comfort her, he narrowly stopped himself from taking her in his arms and holding her, knowing she would react with horror.

When she could finally talk, she croaked, "I fail to see what is so amusing about my almost drowning."

"Obviously, your ordeal has disarranged your wits, for I think you meant to say, "Thank you for saving me, Mr. Ross. I would have drowned if not for your spectacular bravery in rescuing me. Thank goodness you got here in time. I shall be eternally grateful to you."

Her lips pursed at his sarcasm, yet when she turned those silvery eyes of hers upon him, with water dripping from her long hair and running down her flawless skin, she looked so beautiful, his heart missed a beat.

"I do not mean to seem ungrateful. Of course, I am grateful," she shot back, sounding as ungrateful as anyone he had ever heard.

"But not eternally."

"I just wish—"

"You just wish it was not me who saved you."

Despite her thorough dunking in freezing cold water, her cheeks flushed with the heat of embarrassment.

Surprised at how disappointed her reaction made him feel, he sighed. "I see I've hit the nail on the head. It's all right. I understand. I'm sorry to have inconvenienced you by rescuing you from drowning. I shall certainly think twice next time. But I warn you, you may drown whilst I am wasting time summoning more acceptable assistance."

"A duck flew up behind me and took me by surprise. That was why I slipped and fell in," she explained huffily, squeezing water from her hair.

"A duck!" Damian could not help the laughter that burst out of him. He slapped his thigh in mirth.

She frowned at him angrily. "That stupid duck almost killed me. What is so funny about that, I would like to know?"

"I apologize for laughing," he muttered, wiping tears from his eyes. "It's— It's quite an amusing picture you paint, that's all. Pray, point out this renegade duck. I will shoot it, we shall eat it for supper, and make sure it cannot reoffend."

"It was a fluke. There will not be a next time," she replied so haughtily, he had to stifle more laughter.

"I admire your certainty, Lady Abby. By the way, you have water weed in your hair," Damian said. Before she could move, he reached over and carefully plucked several strands of the slimy green stuff hurled it away. He was amazed and slightly excited that she allowed him to do it without protest, putting it down to her vulnerability following her ordeal.

"You had better change into dry things soon or you may catch a chill," he advised, genuinely worried for her, yet at the same time secretly admiring the way her soaked gown was clinging to her shapely form.

She scoffed and glanced at the bright sun above, her eyes flashing silver. "On such a hot day as this? I hope I am hardier than that."

Swinging her legs neatly beneath her, she moved to rise. Damian instinctively held out his hand to help her but was unsurprised when she pretended not to have seen it, preferring to struggle by herself, risking her dignity.

He had to smile at her stubbornness, but that quickly turned to concern when her legs would not take her weight as she attempted to get up. It was obvious to him she was trying to conceal how the near-death experience had both shaken her and left her physically weakened.

"Lady Abby, you have not yet fully regained your strength," he said, surprised at how protective he felt towards her. "Pray, do not be stubborn. Take my hand and let me assist you."

With a small huff of annoyance, whether at herself or him, he could not tell, she gave in and grasped his hand. She had lost her gloves in the water, and when their bare, damp skin touched, Damian had to stifle a gasp of shock. The same strange jolt as before suddenly shot up his arm, as though lightning had arced between them. At the same moment, he felt a tremor pass through her and knew she had felt it too.

They stared at each other for a frozen moment, their eyes and hands locked together. A storm of emotions flickered fleetingly across hers: confusion, fear, and something else he could not identify. God only knew what she saw in him, for he found himself loath to let go of her hand. Small, fine-boned, exquisitely soft, it nestled in his large palm like a tiny bird, a novel sensation that stoked his sudden urge to protect her.

Whatever it was she saw in his expression, it must have frightened her. She hastily broke their gaze and pulled her hand from his, breaking the spell.

"Thank you," she murmured, turning away from him, but not quite fast enough to hide her blushes.

Why does it feel so good to make her blush? he wondered, his heart skipping another beat. *I've seen hundreds of ladies blush in my time, but it's never made me feel like this before.*

"My boots," she said, looking forlornly at where they were floating in the water.

"I'll get them." He strode back into the lake and fetched the sodden boots and handed them to her. She upended them, and water ran out.

"Thank you." She turned and, clutching the boots, began plodding wearily across the lawn in her wet, stockinged feet, back towards the house.

"I simply cannot allow you to walk with bare feet, Lady Abby," Damian insisted, hurriedly flinging on his coat and pulling on his own boots before following her. "You might cut your feet on something sharp, and I would never forgive myself."

"I'm quite all right, I assure— eek! What are you doing?!" she cried as Damian scooped her up in his arms and carried her, striding along, secretly relishing the feeling of her soft, warm weight lying against him. "I'm being a gentleman and protecting you from injury," he replied, enjoying himself.

"I do not need your protection. Please, put me down! I insist on walking," she protested, wriggling to escape. But his arms held her, and he was determined not to let her go.

"I'm afraid I must insist on carrying you back to the house. Think what Ralph would say if I allowed any harm to come to you."

She tried her usual cold, imperious approach, saying angrily, "Mr. Ross, this is an outrage. I demand you put me down this instant!"

"Please do not try to dissuade me from my duty to safeguard you, Lady Abby. It's a matter of masculine honor," he replied, caught up in the marvelous sensation of having her arms around his neck, of looking right into those gorgeous silver-grey eyes, of having her lips only inches from his.

"Masculine honor? What nonsense. What about my feminine pride? You are simply taking advantage of the fact that you are bigger and stronger than I and can pick me up and carry me along like a … like a sack of turnips, against my wishes. What is so gentlemanly or honorable about that?"

Laughter bubbled up from deep within Damian and burst out before he could stop it. "Priceless, utterly priceless," he muttered as they went up the steps to the terrace at the rear of the house. There, the French doors stood open onto the drawing room, lace curtains fluttering in the warm breeze.

A small, adorable frown appeared on her smooth brow. "There you go again, laughing at me!" she cried fiercely.

"Well, how can I help it when you insist on being so comical? Comparing yourself to a sack of turnips! If I had done that, I'm sure you would have slapped my face!" he chortled, unable to contain his mirth.

"I feel like slapping it now!" she declared, her eyes blazing. However, some obscure part of him noticed with odd satisfaction that she did not remove her arms from his neck.

"Go ahead. I would prefer a show of passion to the usual stony silence," he taunted her.

"Oh! You are ... you are insufferable. Let me down, I say!" She promptly let go of his neck and beat ineffectually at his chest with her small fists.

Damian spluttered with helpless laughter as they reached the French doors. "I'm about to, Lady Abby. And I shall leave you here with a clear conscience, knowing I have delivered your feet to the safety of plush Turkey carpet in a suitably thoughtful and gentlemanly manner."

He set her down at the threshold of the drawing room, expecting her to flounce inside in high dudgeon. But instead, she stood looking up at him, a small puddle forming around her feet.

"Is this where you slap my face?" he teased, flinching as she suddenly raised her hand as though to strike him. But it was a feint because she merely pushed a wet hank of hair behind her ear. The playful, childish trick surprised him. He had no idea she had it in her and was more intrigued than ever.

Chapter Nine

At that moment, something caught Damian's eye. Between the strands of dripping auburn hair, a patch of ruched, red skin was visible on one side of Abby's neck, just below her ear.

A scar? How did she get that? he wondered with mild curiosity. But then, people who worked with horses often have scars, from falls and suchlike. He had a nasty one on his lower back from a hunting accident. It was an occupational hazard, so he thought little of it. When she moved slightly, it disappeared from view, and he promptly forgot about it.

"I would appreciate it if you did not mention to Ralph that I fell in the lake and almost drowned. I do not wish to worry him unnecessarily," she suddenly said.

"My lips are sealed." Enjoying sparring with her, he pantomimed locking them and throwing away the imaginary key. "Are you sure you're all right? Don't need any more help?" he added with mocking solicitousness, keen to provoke her fiery temper again for his own amusement.

She lifted her chin with a hint of defiance which, considering her comically bedraggled appearance, had Damian smiling again.

"I'm quite all right, and I require no more assistance from you," she replied archly before pausing for a moment, as though steeling herself to say something unpleasant. "Thank you for saving my life. I'm very grateful to you. But it does not change anything between us. I still do not want you here, and I still think you're an insufferable boor."

Then, with a toss of her dripping hair, she disappeared indoors.

Well, she pulls no punches. At least I know where I stand, Damian thought, chuckling to himself as he made his way to his chambers to dry off and change.

However, while he was doing that, a memory popped into his mind that shook him out of his light-hearted mood. He suddenly found himself back by the lake, in the moment when he had realized it was Abby in the water, screaming in panic and shouting for help.

Of course, he would have done his best to save anyone in that position. But he doubted he would have felt the same gut-wrenching terror as he had at that moment. It had felt as though his heart had literally leaped into his mouth, and the need to save her or perish in the attempt had been overwhelming. He had never experienced anything like it before.

What if I hadn't happened to pass by the lake at that moment? he asked himself, his blood suddenly turning as cold as the lake water. *What if no one had heard her screams?*

He shuddered. It did not bear thinking about. It dawned on him then that he did not want anything bad to happen to Lady Abby. Not ever. Not if he could prevent it.

This was both mystifying and troubling because it felt as if he were not in charge of his own feelings, that some outside force was manipulating him, and there was not a blasted thing he could do about it. Moreover, he was not sure he wanted to.

I must be going mad, he thought, bewildered by his contrariness. *How can I possibly feel that way about a woman who snubs me every chance she gets? Who has made it crystal clear that she wants me gone and thinks me an insufferable boor? And she's ungrateful into the bargain. What is the matter with me?*

He gave himself a hard mental shake to disrupt the unsettling trend of his thoughts and feelings. But the next minute, while he was combing his hair in the washstand mirror, Abby's delicate, ethereally pale face appeared in his mind, her quick-silver eyes shining, water streaming down her cheeks.

He paused, the comb poised in mid-air, briefly reliving the intense pleasure of having her in his arms as he carried her back to the house, of feeling her slender arms around his neck, her small, perfectly formed rosy lips close enough to kiss. *By God, she's lucky I'm such a gentleman!*

He recalled the moment by the French doors, when she had played a trick on him, fooling him into thinking she was about to slap him. There had been a flicker of mischief in her eyes then, revealing a playful side to her he would never have believed existed ... and which belied her words.

"I still do not want you here, and I still think you're an insufferable boor."

"Methinks the lady doth protest too much," he muttered, remembering his Shakespeare, giving up on trying to tame his unruly hair.

But just as he was about to go and seek out Ralph to talk business, he was suddenly seized by a sort of panic. *I'm letting her get under my skin, exactly what I should not be doing. I should be sticking to my principles—no entanglements—and consider myself lucky she hates me. I need to keep it that way.*

* * *

"It was so humiliating, Maude. And the worst thing is, I must now be grateful to Mr. Ross for rescuing me. Oh, it's too vexing!" a disgruntled Abby told Maude's reflection in the vanity mirror later that afternoon.

They were in her chambers, and she was seated at the vanity, having recently gotten out of a hot bath. Maude was standing behind her, combing out her freshly washed hair.

"Is that so bad, Milady? He's such a nice gentleman, and I for one am very glad he happened along to save you," Maude said with a shudder.

"Well, obviously, I'm glad to be alive," Abby replied, deliberately downplaying the seriousness of her near-death experience and, therefore, Damian's heroism. In fact, while thrashing in the lake, her lungs rapidly filling with what felt like gallons of foul-tasting water, she had sincerely believed she was about to die.

Considering the many times she had wished she had perished in the fire rather than live with her scars, she had been surprised by how hard she had fought for life. She had a hard time admitting it to herself, but Damian had appeared at her side like an angel sent from God to save her at the last minute.

So much so, she had thought she must be hallucinating. The overwhelming relief and gratitude she had felt when his strong arms enclosed her and he carried her from the lake would be a secret she would take to the grave. Or so she told herself.

"But why did it have to be him?" she went on, resolutely denying the truth. "And he was so pleased with himself for it, too. That's why he kept laughing at me, because he knows I'm beholden to him forever now." She frowned before adding doubtfully, "At least, I think that's why he was laughing. In any case, how shall I face him at dinner tonight? I do not trust him to keep his promise not to tell Ralph." She paused to sigh. "Ralph will have a fit worrying that I almost died. He'll start fussing over me, and Mr. Ross will be laughing at me up his sleeve."

"I'm sure he won't, Milady," Maude replied with a smile Abby knew was meant to be reassuring but failed to hit the mark. "He's far too gentlemanly for that."

"Oh, yes he will, mark my words," Abby replied, prickling at the mention of "gentlemanly" behavior, feeling she had had quite enough of that from her arch nemesis already. "But Ralph will be grateful to Mr. Ross as well, and he'll expect me to fawn all over the dratted man in gratitude, no doubt. To think I have to spend the whole day with him at the horse fair. Honestly, I cannot tell you how much I am dreading it."

She certainly was fearful about being amongst so many people again. But that fear paled into insignificance next to the fear of being alone with Damian for so long and actually having to talk and cooperate with him over the purchases of the horses.

But deep down, she knew her fear had less to do with his being an unwelcome stranger whom Ralph had inflicted upon her, and more because he was warm and funny and clever. And he loved horses.

As if that combination were not hard enough to resist, he also happened to be strong, tall, and athletically built, with unruly dark hair that flopped appealingly across his forehead, green eyes that were alternately warm and piercing, and a smile that made her heart race whenever she saw it. In short, an admirable male specimen.

And now, I owe him my life.

She recalled the intense moment of closeness they had shared by the lake, when the world around them had suddenly seemed to shrink until it was just the two of them inside a bubble. The longing for him to kiss her had been so terrifying, she had forced herself to break the spell for fear of what might happen if she did not.

And now, it's going to be so much harder to resist being nice to him. It's so unfair! How on earth shall I maintain distance between us for a whole day? Thank goodness I shall have Maude with me to ease the tension. Otherwise, I think I shall go mad!

"Speaking of that, Milady, since we'll be making an early start in the morning, we should discuss what you wish to wear so I can get it ready for you this evening," Maude said in a way that made Abby suspect she had deliberately changed the subject. But whether she had or not, the maid was right.

Frightened by the feminine instinct to look pretty for Damian that surged within her, before she could surrender to it, Abby replied quickly, "It is a horse fair. Something plain and practical will do."

"But, Milady, there will be people there!" Maude exclaimed, her eyes widening in consternation. "What will they say about you if your appearance is not up to par?"

"I'm not looking forward to being among all those people at all, Maude. It makes me feel ill to think of it, and I am only glad you will be there too. But it's hardly going to be *le haute monde*, is it? We're talking about a local horse fair, not Tattersall's at Hyde Park Corner," Abby retorted, citing London's elite horse repository where wealthy, fashionable gentlemen flocked to purchase horses, vehicles, and all related paraphernalia.

Trying her hardest to convince herself for Ralph's sake, she went on, "There won't be many women there at all, and certainly no grand ladies of the *Ton* visiting from London. No one important will be there to recognize me, I'm sure."

Though she spoke confidently, inwardly, she was far from it. Her fear of going out in public among a crowd of strangers was already in full swing. Her terror of possibly bumping into someone of the *Ton* who recognized her and remembered why she had withdrawn from society was greater still. The wounds caused by the *Ton's* past cruel judgement had opened up again and felt fresh and raw.

Add to that the pressure of having to spend all day keeping Damian at arm's length, and I am a nervous wreck!

"I hope you're right about that, Milady," Maude said, the worried edge to her voice only making Abby doubt her own words more.

"Well, I am as certain as I can be," she said. "But I think it would be helpful to dress as plainly as possible, so as not to draw attention. Ideally, I should look like a farmer's wife, respectable but practical."

"Not your usual divided skirts then, Milady?" Maude said, tittering mischievously.

Abby had to smile at the picture of widespread outrage the maid's suggestion conjured. "Very amusing, Maude. If I wanted to cause a riot then, yes, that would be perfect. But on this occasion, a farmer's wife it must be if you please. It will be a sort of disguise, which I hope will help me not to feel so nervous being in a crowd."

They spent a little while assembling the dullest outfit they could find in Abby's wardrobe, which proved quite a challenge. In the end, they settled on a well-used, high-waisted riding habit of bottle green which they unearthed from a chest full of clothing she no longer wore.

Once they had paired it with a plain cotton jabot, or neckcloth, to conceal her scars, leather gloves, and a black tricorn hat, Abby modelled the outfit in the long looking glass.

"You don't look very much like a dowdy farmer's wife, Milady," Maude remarked, eyeing her mistress' stunning reflection skeptically. "But it's the only thing approaching "respectable and serviceable" we can find at such short notice."

"It is perfect," Abby declared, satisfied. "I look quite dull and unremarkable."

She did not notice the way Maude rolled her eyes and shook her head then, as if to say, "Fool yourself if you wish, Milady, but prepare to be disappointed."

Chapter Ten

With her nerves already jangling at the prospect of tomorrow's ordeal, Abby had to stop and take a deep breath to steel herself before going into Ralph's chambers, not knowing what to expect. Even after the conversation with Maude, she was still very confused about how she should feel about Damian saving her from drowning and how she should act in his presence.

She decided it would depend on whether Damian had told Ralph about it or not. In a way, she hoped he had because then she could be justifiably angry with him for breaking his promise to keep her secret. Anger made it easier to maintain her distance from him.

But what if he has kept his promise and not told him? Then, I shall have to be grateful to him for that as well as saving my life! And how will I do that without being nice to him?

When she went in, the two men were talking quietly and drinking wine, but broke off to greet her. Ralph was leaning against his pillows, his plastered leg sticking out of the covers incongruously. But her eye was immediately drawn to Damian, who was standing next to the bed.

He, too, had changed out of his wet clothes, and Abby's heart skipped a beat to see him looking every inch the elegant gentleman in his perfectly tailored evening clothes. In fact, he seemed to have grown even more handsome in the few hours since they had parted.

But that cannot be possible, she told herself with something like despair. *It must be that this wretched attraction I feel for him is growing stronger and making it seem that way.*

Hiding her disquiet, she smiled at Ralph as she went over to kiss his cheek, making sure to stand on the opposite side of the bed from Damian. "Good evening, Brother, dear. How are you faring? Is the leg giving you much pain still?" she asked with concern.

"Pain isn't the word, old girl. It's agony," he declared with a cheeriness that belied his claim. "And you can't imagine how frustrating it is not being able to walk anywhere but have to be carried about like a helpless invalid."

"Like a sack of turnips, perhaps?" Damian inquired casually, catching Abby's eye. A giggle immediately rose up within her, but she pushed it down. To laugh at the shared joke would, she felt, encourage him and tempt disaster.

Ralph laughed and lifted his glass to his friend. "If you like, old fellow, yes, a veritable sack of turnips," he agreed. To Abby he said, "You are precisely three minutes late. Father would not have been pleased. Now, hurry up and sit down, will you? I'm starving, and I want my dinner."

Abby genuinely laughed, feigning penitence. "I humbly beg your pardon, Brother. To think you might have starved to death in those three minutes. How shall I ever atone for my crime?"

"I'll think of something when I get this blasted plaster cast off my leg," he assured her before explaining to a puzzled-looking Damian about the running jest between them that made fun of their father.

"He was an absolute demon for punctuality. If either of us appeared for a meal so much as a second after the appointed time, we'd get a stern telling off, wouldn't we, Abby?"

"Well, you certainly did, many times. I learned the lesson early and made sure not to be late," she replied teasingly, glad to see him in good spirits despite his predicament.

"Only because you used to hide in the sideboard in the dining room and read your book for an hour while you waited for dinner to arrive," Ralph accused her good-naturedly.

"You are only saying it like that because you are jealous you did not think of it first," she countered, burningly conscious of Damian's eyes upon her. She could hardly believe she was laughing and joking in front of him, letting him get a glimpse of her true personality. Frustratingly, there seemed to be a traitorous part of her that had taken over control of her body and craved his attention.

"Nonsense. I was just far too big to fit in the sideboard," Ralph declared, cackling with laughter.

"If you are referring to your head then, yes, I have to agree," she replied, feeling odd when Damian laughed too.

She was settling Ralph's dinner tray on his lap when she realized he knew nothing of what had occurred that afternoon at the lake. It seemed that, like the perfect gentleman he so annoyingly kept on proving himself to be, Damian had kept his promise.

Abby's traitorous heart warmed to him even further, and she hardly dared glance his way for fear she might smile at him. She felt increasingly like a child who is fascinated by fire and cannot resist putting her fingers into the flames, even knowing they would burn her.

When she turned around, half hoping Damain would have fetched his own tray and she could avoid handing it to him, she saw he was waiting by her chair, tray in hand.

"Do sit down and allow me to serve your dinner, Lady Abby," he said smoothly, giving her no choice but to do as he asked or appear openly rude.

"Thank you, Mr. Ross," she murmured, sitting down, taking special care that their fingers did not touch when she took the tray from him. However, she caught a waft of his manly scent mixed with fresh, lemony cologne, and her heart sank a little. Because it was by far the most delicious thing she could ever recall smelling.

"My pleasure, Lady Abby, and I do wish you would call me Damian," he replied, fetching his own dinner and resuming his seat. "We shall be living under the same roof for a long time, I hope, so there seems little point in maintaining such formalities."

Absolutely not. Formality is just about all that is holding me together!

She forced herself to meet his penetrating gaze, which seemed to drill into her as if he would read her thoughts. "That is a kind invitation," she told him, masking her unease with a coldness she did not feel. "However, I am afraid that, unlike yourself, I am a stickler for formality, *Mr. Ross*."

Ralph burst out laughing. "Oh, she's in fine form this evening. I believe she's getting used to you, Damian, old chap. You'd better watch out. Our Abby has a sharp tongue and an even sharper mind," he warned his friend before spooning more white soup into his mouth.

"I have already discovered that, my friend," Damian admitted, a strange flicker in his eyes as he smiled warmly across at her. It was such a lovely smile. Abby's heart fluttered madly, and she hurriedly looked down at her plate. Because she feared that if she did not, she would smile back at him.

And that would spell disaster!

* * *

"Twenty-five miles in just under two hours, with only two changes of horses on the way," Damian said conversationally to Abby as he handed her down from the barouche when they arrived at the Stoughton horse fair. "But that's with dry, reasonably good roads, of course."

"Thank you," she said stiffly, ignoring his remarks about the journey and snatching her hand from his as soon as her little booted feet hit the ground. It told him she had also felt the strange little spark that always passed between them whenever they touched. But whereas he found it intriguing and exciting, predictably, she appeared to hate it.

Of course, she does, because she hates me.

He told himself he had no idea why he was bothering to try talking to her at all. She had hardly spoken to him for the entire journey and avoided looking at him unless forced to. She had occupied herself with whispering to Maude or staring out of the window, a small frown fixed between her brows, her fingers constantly twisting in her lap.

She seems very nervous. Or perhaps she isn't nervous but angry at having to endure my presence for so long. Oh, well, it's no more than I expected. I must put a brave face on things, I suppose, but it does not bode well for a successful outcome to the day.

"Crowded, isn't it?" he observed, offering his hand to Maude to help her alight. Unlike her mistress, the maid repaid him for his assistance with a warm smile. "It's a good thing we've arrived early," he added, as expected receiving no acknowledgement from Abby.

The driver went off to find a place to park, and they stood for a few moments, looking out over the milling sea of people and horses. Damian breathed in the delightful aroma of humanity, hay, and horse manure as he took a moment to admire Abby.

He thought she stood out from the crowd effortlessly in her smart green riding habit, her auburn hair pinned beneath a tricorn hat. It gave her a sort of rakish look he found very appealing. He felt stupidly good walking about the place with such a beautiful woman at his side, even if she despised him. He noticed with an unaccountable flash of irritation that she was drawing appreciative looks from many passing gentlemen.

Most of the ladies of his acquaintance would have been preening to garner such male attention, so he was puzzled by tense look of barely suppressed fear on her face.

"Milady hates crowds," Maude whispered to him covertly before going to link her arm through Abby's, who clung to it as if it were a life raft in a stormy sea.

Of course! She doesn't like strangers, does she? And this place is full of them. No wonder she looks so nervous. I wonder at Ralph for inflicting this on her, knowing how difficult it must be. I could easily have come alone, so what is he playing at, I wonder? I suppose he must have his reasons.

Feeling his protective instincts roused but knowing that any demonstration of them would be summarily rejected, he said to himself, *I must look after her, without seeming to, of course, and make her feel more at ease. I should like her to enjoy the day, even if she has to spend it with an insufferable bore like me.*

"Well, ladies, the sale does not start until eleven, and it is only just past ten. I suggest we get out of this crowd and go and have some tea to fortify ourselves before we start on the serious business of buying horses."

The look of relief on Abby's face was heartwarming and told him he was on the right track.

"Yes, the journey was quite long. I should like a cup of tea," she said in a small voice, the longest sentence he had heard her speak so far that day.

He found them a quiet corner to sit in the refreshments marquee and ordered tea for three. Well aware she would not respond to any attempt at small talk, he drew the sale catalogue from his coat pocket and handed it to her.

"I've marked a few of the horses I think we should look at. I'm interested to know your opinion on them," he said, then withdrew to drink his tea quietly while she perused the pages with deep concentration.

Meanwhile, he exchanged a look with Maude, who gave a subtle nod of approval. He felt he had a friend in the maid, and his gratitude towards her abounded. He ordered cakes to be brought and made sure she got one for herself and also insisted she have the one which, he guessed rightly, Abby would refuse.

He almost choked on a mouthful of cake with surprise when Abby suddenly looked up from the catalogue and spoke to him in a forthright manner, all traces of her former fear gone.

"I think you have made a worthy selection, Mr. Ross. All of those you have marked are definitely worth looking at. I particularly like the look of these two colts, the gray Arabian and the thoroughbred chestnut." She held out the catalogue and indicated the entries on the page with her gloved finger. "Both have excellent lineages, and if they are as described, have a lot of potential. I think we should look at them first."

Damian hurriedly swallowed the cake and recovered his composure. "Ah, yes, they do rather stand out, don't they?" he replied, secretly thrilled she was talking to him as if he were a human being for the first time and even agreed with his selection. He had expected her to disagree on principle, simply because it was him. "However, the prices quoted seem a little high."

"They do, but perhaps the sellers will be open to a little bargaining."

Well, well, well. So, she's not so shy as to be averse to a little haggling, is she? "We shall soon see," he replied, keeping his excitement firmly in check. "Do you think Ralph would approve if we got them both?"

She nodded. "If they live up to expectations, I am certain he would. But as you say, we must wait and see."

"Very well, then, Lady Abby. I'm glad you approve of my choices. We shall do as you suggest and start with the two colts."

"Good. The sooner we make our purchases, the sooner we can leave." She eyed the gathering throng inside the marquee uneasily over the rim of her cup.

Damian realized that though she was afraid of being out in a crowd like this, she cared enough about choosing the right horses for the business to try to overcome it. He admired her bravery and felt a new respect for her because of it. However, he still could not help wondering why she was so afraid of strangers and crowds. *Has she always been that way?* he wondered. *Or did something happen to make her like that?*

Chapter Eleven

At any rate, she's talking to me, and that's encouraging, Damian told himself.

But when they left the marquee just before eleven and stepped out into the throng, Lady Abby looked so fearful and clung so hard to Maude's arm, he became concerned and resorted to a little subterfuge to try to put her more at ease.

Looking at the crowd with mild distaste, he put on his hat and remarked, "I do wish there were not so many people here. Such crowds make me feel uneasy. Do you not find it so, Lady Abby?"

Her head snapped up, and he was surprised by the suspicion in her eyes.

"Are you mocking me, Mr. Ross," she asked icily.

"Mocking you, Lady Abby?" he asked in confusion, realizing he had blundered in some way. "I don't understand. Have I said something to offend you?"

She stared at him a moment longer before the suspicion faded and her cheeks reddened slightly. "I was merely surprised to hear you say you dislike crowds, that is all," she replied. "Ralph gave me to understand that you are at ease in such social situations as this. You are good at talking to people, I think he said. Perhaps he is wrong about that."

Ah, this is to do with Ralph choosing me as his partner over her. It must be because I can deal with people easily and she cannot. That's why she thought I was mocking her, he suddenly realized.

He sought to brush it off and minimize any damage. "No, he's not wrong. But talking to sellers and breeders and so on at events such as this does not mean one has to be comfortable with crowds. It's usually a one-to-one affair."

"I suppose so," she replied in the same quiet way, looking nervously around at the growing crush. "At any rate, crowds can certainly be rather intimidating at times. If you do not mind, I would like to go and look at the horses now."

"If that is what you wish, then by all means," he replied, starting to get a better idea of the extent of her uneasiness in the crowded public place.

For that reason, when they headed for the seller's paddock in search of the two colts they had earmarked, he went ahead, carving a path for her through the growing press of people and horses.

She kept her head down and stayed glued to Maude's side until they eventually reached the gate. Damian found himself wishing it was his arm she was clinging to for safety rather than the maid's, then silently chided himself for being a fool.

On inspection, the two colts proved to be as promising as they hoped, and they quickly concluded the purchases at a good price and arranged for the horses to be delivered to Worsley as soon as possible.

Damian was pleased things had gone so well and would not have minded lingering a while longer at the event, having journeyed so long to get there. But now that their business was concluded, Abby was intent on leaving. Having no wish to make things worse for her, he went along with it.

But on the way back to the barouche, as he was leading the two women through the crowd, Damian spied something above the sea of heads that made his blood boil.

A man in scruffy clothing was beating a horse, a white mare with speckling of dark spots on her nose. The poor thing looked weak and skinny from underfeeding, her coat and eyes dull. She was whinnying in pain and trying to avoid the blows as the man yanked hard on the rope halter and repeatedly lashed at her flanks.

Anger surged through Damian. If one thing made him lose his temper it was seeing defenseless animals, particularly horses, mistreated. He turned to Abby and Maude and said, "Excuse me for a moment, ladies, there's something I must attend to urgently."

Leaving them standing, he pushed his way quickly through the crowd, reached the fellow wielding the whip, and snatched it roughly from his hand.

"How would you like to feel that whip upon your cheek, you low-witted bounder?" he ground out, looming over the man, raising the whip threateningly.

"Oi! Who d'you think you are?! Give me back that whip. That's my property, that is! And you've no right to take it from a fella like that," the man protested belligerently, wheeling around to see his assailant.

He took one look at Damian and his demeanor abruptly changed. He tore off his ragged cap and cowered obsequiously. "Sorry, Guvnor, I didn't mean nothin' by it. She's a lazy old screw, stubborn as anythin' she is, can't get her to do anythin' without a good whackin'," he whined in justification of his cruelty.

"If I were her, I wouldn't do anything for you either, you miserable excuse for a cur. Perhaps if you fed her and didn't beat her, she might be more amenable. You're lucky she hasn't kicked your thick head off by now." He snapped the whip in two and threw it at the man. "There's your whip back."

"How much?" A soft feminine voice suddenly came from behind him, taking him by surprise. He turned his head and saw Abby standing next to him, her silvery gaze fixed on the man. The fellow's eyes grew round as he stared at her. Maude stood behind her, looking on grimly.

"I asked you a question," Abby said haughtily to the man. "You will be so good as to answer me. How much for the horse?" She gestured at the undernourished mare with her chin.

The man's eyes lit up with greed, clearly seeing an opportunity to rook a rich lady.

"Fifty pounds, lady," he said, his grin revealing blackened teeth.

"I'll give you twenty-five."

"Forty-five. She's a good 'orse."

"You just told me she's a lazy screw," Damian pointed out angrily, ready to punch the fellow.

"Twenty-five pounds," Abby countered, as cool as a cucumber. Though still seething at the man, Damian had to admire both her acumen and her determination to save the horse from further misery. He had intended to do the same, but she had forestalled him.

"Forty, and not a penny less, lady."

"Twenty-five. And you can throw in the halter." Abby held out the banknotes. The sight proved too much for the man.

He spat on the ground. "You drive a hard bargain, lady. All right, twenny-five it is." He snatched the money and squirreled it away about his grimy person before handing her the halter. "She's all yours and good riddance," he said. Hitching up his trousers, he walked away in the direction of the ale tent.

"What an absolute swine," Damian exhaled, his fury draining away as he watched the fellow depart. When he looked at Abby, she already had a reassuring hand on the mare's neck and was petting her nose and whispering into her ear. The poor beast nickered softly and rubbed its head against hers as though in gratitude.

"That was well done, Mr. Ross," Abby said, looking up and meeting his eyes. Their unexpected warmth coupled with her brilliant smile set his heart thumping in his chest. It was the first time she had ever smiled at him, and it seared him like a flame.

"I cannot abide cruelty to animals," he told her sincerely. "It was probably a good thing you intervened when you did, or I should likely have beat that miserable blackguard into the ground and been arrested by the constables."

"Then I am glad we got here in time," she replied, still smiling and petting the horse. "Seeing as you are her savior, would you like to stroke her?"

"Indeed, the poor lass," he said, taking her up on the invitation and going to run his hands along the mare's flanks, carefully avoiding the raised welts where the man had whipped her. "Look, she's been starved as well as beaten, see how her ribs are sticking out," he added, frowning.

"Thanks to you, she shall never know hunger again, nor the lash of the whip," Abby said, an edge of admiration to her voice. "You shall have a new home now, darling, and you need never be afraid of anything again," she told the mare, planting a small kiss on its nose.

Damian was moved by the sweet gesture. He realized this was the real Abby Lucas he was seeing, and he liked it more than he knew was good for him.

"I do not know her name. What shall you call her?" he asked.

"Alba, for her white coat," she replied.

"An excellent choice." He nodded approvingly. "Now, how shall we get her home?"

"We shall drop her off at the inn when we change horses on the way home and send someone back to fetch her tomorrow."

She has it all worked out, just like that.

"Very well. I shall pay the grooms well to give her a good feed and make sure she's comfortable until then," he replied. "It will be some time before she recovers from her mistreatment. What shall you do with her?"

She smiled at him slightly quizzically. "Why, I shall let her be a horse, of course. What else?"

She laughed and so did Maude. Damian joined in, delighted that the barriers seemed to be coming down at last. Indeed, now she had Alba, and perhaps also because she knew they would shortly be heading home, Abby seemed much more relaxed. It truly warmed his heart to see it.

Alba was content to follow her new mistress, who led her by the halter as they made their way slowly through the crowd, heading to the field where the barouche waited.

By now, it was noon, and the sun was high overhead, beating down on all below. Feeling the effects, when Damian caught sight of a stand selling fruit ices, he asked Abby and Maude if they would like one. They both accepted eagerly, and Maude was dispatched to join the queue.

While they waited, he and Abby had a perfectly civilized conversation about how old Alba might be and what diet would be best to bring her up to full condition.

They were both so engrossed that neither of them noticed the two women until they heard a loud voice behind him say, "Well, bless my soul, if it isn't Lady Abby Lucas. Long time, no see. Fancy meeting you here!"

Damian saw Abby start and panic flare in her eyes as they shot immediately to the owner of the voice. He turned and saw a short, fair-haired young woman with a large bosom, round face, and a smile that did not reach her dark blue eyes. She was wearing an expensive-looking outfit he thought was overdone for the occasion.

Her companion was taller, thinner, dark-haired, and clad in a pale-yellow costume that did her pallid complexion no favors. Two young maids loitered behind them at a distance, looking miserable.

"L-Lady Araminta, L-Lady June," Abby stuttered, a strained smile appearing on her lips. "What a pleasant surprise. How nice to see you both."

Instantly, Damian knew the encounter was a far from a pleasant surprise for her. In fact, judging by the change in her demeanor, it was quite the opposite. She looked terrified, and his protective instincts surged one more.

"How nice indeed," replied Lady Araminta, eyeing him curiously down her nose.

"Yes, it is a long time since we have run into each other, Lady Abby," Lady June put in with a thin smile, her dark eyes sweeping assessingly over Abby from head to toe. "I believe the last time we met was at the Frazer's ball. That would have been ... let me see ..."

"Four years ago," Lady Araminta supplied. "And we have not seen you at all during the Season since then. Pray tell, where have you been hiding all this time?"

"I-I have not been hiding, only spending time at home in the country. I-I prefer it there to the town," Abby replied, her voice unsteady.

Damian frowned, wondering what the matter was. *If the ladies are not strangers, then why is she so frightened?*

Chapter Twelve

The ladies tittered at Abby's response, and Damian watched as her cheeks flushed scarlet.

"How refreshingly candid of you. I know very few ladies who would admit to that," Araminta declared, her eyebrows shooting up to her hairline.

"Indeed, I have seldom heard of such a thing," June said, nodding in agreement with her friend. "How original you are, Lady Abby! I admit, I start to go mad after a week in the country. I have to be in town, or I should simply die."

Abby did not respond, but seemed to Damian to be putting all her effort into keeping the polite smile pinned to her face. One look in her eyes told him she wished the ground would open up and swallow her. He decided to intervene and doffed his hat to the women, giving them each a small bow.

"Good afternoon to you, ladies. Forgive me for butting in, but I feel I am at a disadvantage in not having made your acquaintance. Allow me to introduce myself. I am Damian Ross, Lady Abby's escort for the day." Abby's lack of response to his outrageous claim made him certain something was wrong.

"Good day to you, Mr. Ross, charmed, I'm sure," said Araminta, batting her eyelashes at him as she offered her gloved hand for him to kiss and dropped a small curtsey.

"How do you do, Mr. Ross? I am pleased to meet you," June told him with a sly smile, following suit. She scrutinized him closely. "Do you know, you look somehow familiar to me. Have we met before?"

"I'm sure I would remember if I had had that pleasure, my lady," Damian replied, silently praying she would not recognize him for who he really was. Thankfully, her friend intervened and distracted her.

"Oh, June, how silly of me," Araminta suddenly exclaimed laughingly. "I have only just remembered why Lady Abby is no longer seen about town. I apologize, Lady Abby, if my earlier remarks caused any offence. My head is like a feather pillow sometimes!"

Damian frowned. *What is she talking about?*

"What do you mean, Minty, dear?" June asked, her thin brows beetling.

"Oh, you know," her friend replied and whispered something in her ear.

June stared at Abby, her eyes growing wide. "Oh, of course, yes. I had forgotten all about that. In that case, it is quite understandable that you would prefer to remain in the country, Lady Abby. I should want to do the same in your shoes, to avoid any unpleasantness, I'm sure."

"Oh, absolutely," Araminta agreed. "It is very wise of you in the circumstances, Abby, dear. I mean to say, it would be heartbreaking to participate in the Season if one had no hope of making a match."

What? What on earth does the cheeky chit mean by that? Damian wondered, stunned by the underhanded rudeness of the comment and seriously concerned to see its effect on Abby. Her face turned deathly pale beneath the red flush, and, if he was not mistaken, she was trembling.

"Are you feeling unwell, Lady Abby?" he asked worriedly. "You seem to have gone very pale."

"Um, yes, I fear I am unwell and feeling a little faint, Mr. Ross. I think I must sit down," she replied, swaying slightly and putting her hand on his arm for support.

That uncharacteristic touch told him all he needed to know. *I have to get her away from these two insolent baggages before she swoons!*

"Do excuse us, ladies," he told them bluntly. "I must escort Lady Abby to a seat forthwith. I fear something in the air disagrees with her. Good day to you both."

Without waiting for a response, he took hold of Alba's halter and tucked Abby's arm in his. She accepted it without demur and allowed him to lead her along with the horse to a bench shaded by a tree. He made her sit down and tied Alba's halter to a low branch of the tree. The horse bent her head and began munching on the lush grass below.

Before he could say anything to Abby, Maude appeared, clutching three fruit ices in her hands.

"Whatever is the matter, Milady?" the maid asked solicitously, bending over her mistress.

"It happened, Maude. The thing I said would not happen just happened. It was awful," Abby said weakly, pulling her down to sit beside her on the bench.

"Oh, dear. Here, Milady, take this. It will cool you down," Maude said, placing one of the ices into Abby's hand. But she hardly seemed aware of it.

"Mr. Ross, here is yours." He thanked Maude and took the ice she handed him, eating it slowly while taking in the puzzling exchange between the two women.

"Was it those two ladies I saw you talking to?" Maude asked Abby.

Abby nodded limply. "Lady Araminta Greene and Lady June Warrender, two of the biggest gossips in the *Ton*. I cannot believe I could be so unlucky as to run into them."

Maude shuddered. "It was bad luck indeed, but do not take any notice of them. I have heard a thing or two about that Lady Araminta, and none of it good. A friend of mine served as her maid for a while and told me she is very ill-tempered and rude to all the servants. But she can do you no real harm," she added kindly.

Damian was impressed by her obvious affection for her mistress, which he knew had to be earned through kindness and good treatment. *It appears Abby is a good mistress, unlike Lady Araminta,* he concluded. He finished the ice and put the empty glass cup on the end of the bench, continuing to listen to their conversation.

"You did not hear what they said," Abby told the maid, finally seeming to regain some of her color and spirit. The pair proceeded to eat their ices while Abby gave Maude a condensed version of the conversation, both of them acting as if he were not there.

"Pay no mind to them, Milady, they are only jealous because you are so much prettier than they. And they probably thought Mr. Ross was your betrothed and were jealous about that too, him being so handsome and charming," Maude went on.

Damian's brows flew up, startled by the unexpected compliment, which nevertheless made him feel like some sort of ornamental prop.

At last, tired of being kept in the dark, he burst out, "I do wish someone would explain to me what all this is about and why you are so upset, Lady Abby."

Two pairs of eyes looked up at him, one silver, one blue, as if seeing him for the first time.

"I beg your pardon, Mr. Ross, but I came over dizzy all of a sudden, that was all," Abby said, clearly lying through her teeth. "It must be the heat. I thank you for your kind assistance. I am feeling better now and would like to go home if you please."

"But what about those—" he began in frustration, only to be cut off.

"Home, please, Mr. Ross," Abby repeated as Maude helped her up from the bench. She clung to the maid's arm as before.

"Yes, of course," Damian replied, seeing he would get no more out of her. He untied Alba, took hold of her bridle, then led the way through the bustling crowd until they came to the barouche.

Once the women were settled inside, he obtained a long rope from the driver and tied Alba to the back of the vehicle so she could trot along behind them as far as the next inn.

Finally, he climbed inside, and they set off home. This time, it was he who remained silent throughout the journey, stealing secret glances at Abby. She appeared to have recovered her composure, yet looked unhappy and remained sunk in her thoughts throughout the journey.

His mind buzzed with questions as to what exactly had happened back there with the two women, and why she was lying to him about it.

* * *

"He did look very confused and almost angry about it when I had to lie to him about Araminta and June, even though I really did feel dizzy. It is ridiculous, I know, but I feel rather bad about it. Perhaps I should have told him the truth," Abby pondered when she and Maude were closeted safely in her chambers back at Worsley.

"Perhaps, Milady," Maude replied diplomatically. She was helping Abby to change before joining Ralph for dinner in his chambers. Along with Damian, naturally.

"But then I would have had to explain to him exactly why I was so scared to see Araminta and June and why what they said upset me so much …"

"Which would also mean telling him everything else," Maude put in.

"Exactly," Abby agreed decisively. "No, I was right to lie. I do not want him to know about my misfortune. I simply could not stand him to look at me with either pity or revulsion."

"But he might not look at you with either, Milady."

Abby scoffed sadly. "If you had seen the way some gentlemen stared at me in London when they learned of my disfigurement, you would not doubt it, Maude. Besides, whilst I grant Mr. Ross has many good qualities, I shall never be able to truly trust him enough to think of him as a friend." *It would be far too dangerous. Although in truth, it is myself I cannot trust, not him!*

"That is a great shame, Milady, if you don't mind me saying so. For he does have many good qualities," Maude said with a fond smile that had Abby questioning her own decisions even more. "He saved that poor horse, for one. He was so angry, I thought he was going to set about that nasty fellow with the whip!"

"Yes, so did I," Abby murmured, her heart suddenly glowing as she thought back to Damian's heroic defense of poor Alba. "I cannot deny he is very courageous and kind. I have never been so impressed with a gentleman. Even saving me from drowning does not compare to the way he rushed to help poor Alba."

She paused before adding with a deep sense of misgiving, "I confess, in that moment, I felt such an overwhelming surge of affection and gratitude towards him, I simply could not hide it."

"I know, Milady. You could see he was delighted when you smiled at him," Maude answered with obvious approval.

"But that was a bad mistake, Maude!" Abbye exclaimed, genuinely distraught at having let her cold mask slip so many times that day. "Do you not see? I should not have let my guard down like that. The trouble is, he is everything one could ask for in a gentleman, and that is how he is slowly worming his way into my good graces!"

"I can hardly think of a nicer gentleman apart from the master," Maude chimed in.

Frustrated by what felt like the maid's willful lack of understanding, Abby flared up. "Is that supposed to be helpful? Because it is quite the opposite. You ought to be pointing out his bad qualities instead of singing his praises. But I suppose I am foolish to expect anything else, since it is plain you are quite smitten with him!"

Maude took no offence and merely tittered as she fastened the back of Abby's dress. "Not smitten, Milady, but even a lowly girl such as I can admire him from a distance, as I would a lovely painting or one of those statues of heroes from olden times," she replied almost dreamily as she rearranged Abby's lace collar. "I mean, he's so very handsome …"

"Maude! Will you at least pretend to help—" Abby began, but Maude had not finished.

"… That I'm sure he must have ladies chasing after him all the time," she added.

Abby stifled a gasp, horrified by the sharp stab of jealousy she felt in her chest at the idea of Damian being pursued by other ladies. *Beautiful, charming ladies, who are not disfigured like me!*

It was frightening how little control she seemed to have over her feelings when it came to Damian. It felt as though she had involuntarily crossed a line that would lead to calamity.

Nevertheless, she somehow found herself asking, "Do you really think so?"

"I do not doubt it, Milady," Maude replied, steering her flustered mistress over to sit at the stool in front of the vanity and starting to put the finishing touches on her toilette. "And him still single as well. He's quite a catch," she added, apparently oblivious to Abby's consternation.

Abby thrust the jealousy aside and sought safety in sarcasm. "If he is as much of a catch as you say, then why is he still unmarried?" she demanded.

"Who can say, Milady? Perhaps some lady broke his heart, and he has sworn off romance because of it. Perhaps he does not wish to be tied down and prefers the life of a bachelor."

Abby considered both possibilities unlikely. "It seems to me he is the one more likely to go about breaking hearts rather than the other way around," she said almost grudgingly. It struck her then that she knew almost nothing of Damian's background or personal circumstances, and an intense curiosity took hold of her.

But I can hardly ask him about himself and remain aloof at the same time, can I? And if I start asking Ralph questions, he will no doubt assume I have a romantic interest in his friend. That would be too embarrassing. There is simply no way of finding out about him without making a fool of myself. Oh, it is like everything else about him, very frustrating!

Chapter Thirteen

In her struggle to deny the tumult raging inside her, Abby resorted to humor. "Perhaps Mr. Ross simply prefers the company of horses to ladies and thinks them a lot less trouble," she suggested.

"Indeed, Milady, and many horses are far better looking than some ladies I could mention. Lady Araminta Greene, for one," Maude said.

Perhaps because she needed a release from the tension, Abby could not help laughing. "Yes, and they are far nicer too," she said. Then she added, "Speaking of that lady, I was so upset by her spitefulness at the time, I only realized afterwards how dangerously close she was to betraying my secret in front of Mr. Ross. If he had not thought I was ill and whisked me away so quickly, I'm sure she would have gleefully told him all about my unfortunate past."

Maude frowned. "She's not a good person, Milady. It was indeed very lucky Mr. Ross was there and took you away," she said, exchanging Abby's small gold stud earrings for a pair of ruby ones. She then arranged her mistress' hair so that it fell in a mass of auburn ringlets over her shoulder, concealing her scars. "It looks very pretty, Milady," she ventured, admiring her handiwork with a smile.

Abby agreed but with reservations. "Thank you, Maude, that is nicely done, but I am worried that you have made me look too pretty. Remember, I do not want to attract Mr. Ross's attention or make him think I am vying for it."

"I'm sorry, Milady, but it is impossible for you to look anything other than pretty at the very least. Besides, I think it's too late to worry about attracting Mr. Ross's attention. I mean, the way he looks at you ..." She trailed off, letting the unsaid words hang in the air.

Startled, Abby sat up and stared at the maid's reflection in the mirror. "Whatever do you mean?"

"It's obvious he admires you, Milady."

Panicked afresh, Abby burst out, "No, that is nonsense. He cannot admire me. It is quite impossible!" However, amid the panic was a tingle of excitement, and she fleetingly allowed herself to wonder what it might mean if Damian truly did admire her. *What if things were different? What if I did not have these scars? What might happen then?*

The pleasant fantasy was short-lived. Because the logical outcome was not a happy ever after at all. It involved an inevitable rejection followed by heartbreak.

Besides that, because of her disfigurement and society's attitude towards her because of it, she simply did not see herself as worthy of any gentleman's admiration. Especially not one as attractive as Damian.

She shook her head vehemently. "No, you must be mistaken, Maude. If anything, he thinks me rude and ignorant, and it is better that it stays that way."

"If you say so, Milady, but it is going to be very hard to keep pushing him away when he lives in the same house. I mean, he could be here for years," the maid pointed out.

Abby sighed, close to despair. "I know that, and I have no idea how I shall cope. I shall probably go completely mad and have to be shut up in an asylum."

"The master would never allow that, Milady."

"Hmm, that would depend on how mad I am, I suppose. Oh, Maude, I blame myself for forgetting myself in his company today so many times. I laughed and smiled like a fool. I even found myself enjoying conversing with him."

"I did notice, Milady," Maude conceded, dabbing scent behind Abby's ears before giving her reflection a final look of approval. "There, you are ready."

"Thank you, Maude," Abby replied absently, slipping her feet into satin slippers. She was appalled by herself, both for failing to keep her guard up that day and for feeling jealous over some imaginary ladies whom Damian might admire.

"It is simply unfair that he should be so impressive," she bitterly complained. "And that I have so much to be grateful to him for. My life, for a start, and probably Alba's too. I admit I am struggling to stand my ground."

"Then why not give up and just be yourself, Milady?" the maid asked, standing back so Abby could rise.

"You know very well why! If I let myself... Oh, never mind."

Suddenly, she was filled with a familiar sorrow, the kind that came with knowing she was damaged goods. *No gentleman of my choosing will ever love me, I shall never marry or have a family of my own, so it is foolish to dream of it. In fact, it would be best if Damian fell in love with someone else and married them,* she told herself, trying to crush the spark of jealousy the notion sparked. *That would put an end to my stupidity once and for all.*

* * *

Resplendent in a silk dressing gown, Ralph sat propped against his pillows, looking like a cross between a beached whale and an exotic eastern potentate holding court. His court consisted of Abby, seated on one side of the enormous four-poster bed, and Damian on the other. All of them were eating dinner off of trays.

Abby had already been tense upon entering the room, not just from the recent conversation with Maude, but also because she thought Damian was bound to mention to Ralph her being taken ill at the horse fair. Though she had told Ralph it was bound to happen, she did not relish being proved right and disappointing him.

Even if Damian had not filled Ralph in, he was sure to at least ask her how she was feeling. That would alert Ralph's concern, something she did not want. To her surprise, he said nothing about it. But while she appreciated his discretion, it felt awkward to have yet another reason to be grateful to him.

"You have both done splendidly," Ralph declared, tossing the catalogue from the horse fair onto the coverlet and digging into the beef casserole steaming on the plate in front of him. "I could not have made better choices myself. And Abby, Damian says he could not have done it without you. Now, is that not something, coming from an expert like him?"

"From an expert like him, certainly," she replied, disconcerted by the unexpected praise. She glanced across at Damian as if for confirmation.

His smile made her heart turn a somersault in her chest. "When it comes to buying horses, I find it's helpful to have someone else there who knows what they're doing, to discuss the finer points with before deciding to buy," he explained. "In Ralph's absence, you fulfilled that role admirably, Lady Abby."

Confused by the compliment, Abby stared at him, groping in vain for a suitable response. Thankfully, she was saved when Ralph interrupted.

"She probably did better than I would have done if not for this blasted leg," he observed drily. "I like the look of these two new additions," he went on. "They have a lot of promise. Who knows where they might take us in a few years' time? Lifting the trophy at Epsom with any luck."

"If that should come to pass, then we shall have Lady Abby to thank for it as much as either of us, Ralph, old chap. Today, I learned to respect her knowledge and experience when judging horseflesh," Damian said, sounding sincere.

Somehow, Abby managed to keep her composure and reply calmly, "That is kind of you to say, Mr. Ross, but it was you who first picked out the horses. I merely agreed with your selection."

"Which shows we are in perfect accord about what makes a good racehorse," he told her with a nod.

Increasingly unsettled by his seeming determination to compliment her, and by how much she liked it, she countered, "It seems you are bent on flattering me this evening, Mr. Ross. But it is entirely unnecessary, I assure you. I merely did the job I was sent to do to the best of my ability."

"I speak only the truth, Lady Abby," he insisted with an earnestness she found dangerously disarming. "I thought we made a good team today," he added.

Please, Lord, I beg you, make him stop. I cannot stand much more of this flattery. I shall crack and smile at him again, I know I shall!

"A meeting of the minds, eh?" Ralph suggested with a laugh.

Desperate to hide her discomfort, Abby bent over her plate and pushed a piece of potato around with her fork until she could trust herself to speak. "Hardly that, Brother. We simply agreed which horses would be the best investment for the business, that is all."

"Quite so," Damian murmured. Something in his voice made her dare to glance at him. He appeared slightly chastened, and she immediately felt bad about being so dismissive of his kind remarks. *There I go again, being a fool,* she silently chided herself. *I should be glad if I have hurt his feelings. He might actually change the subject now!*

"Well, aside from that, how did you find it today, Abby, dear? Damian says the place was very crowded," Ralph said.

"Yes, it was," she replied warily, not about to admit her fear of being out in public in front of Damian.

"It was rather a crush and very hot as well," Damian remarked, unknowingly coming to her aid by distracting Ralph from further questioning. Besides that, his statement seemed to confirm the truth of his earlier claim to dislike crowds, just as she did. It sparked a strange sense of kinship with him that unsettled her even more.

"And I understand we have acquired another new horse by chance as well, is that so, Abby?" Ralph asked suddenly, smiling at her. "A white mare. Alba, is it?"

The thought of Alba brought a smile unbidden to Abby's lips. "Oh, yes, I paid twenty-five pounds for her," she answered, glad to be on safer ground at last.

"What sort of horse is she?" Ralph inquired.

"Oh, nothing special, but she is very sweet-natured. Once she is up to par, I shall probably ride her myself," she told him.

"She's rather a high stepper, I noticed. Might make a good carriage horse," Damian observed.

"Oh, no!" Abby exclaimed, bristling at the suggestion. "She has worked and suffered enough at that barbarian's hands. I am determined she shall have a life of ease from now on."

"Forgive me. I did not mean to speak out of turn. You are quite right, Lady Abby. She deserves to have a good life," Damian apologized.

"Fair enough, Sister, no need to bite his head off. She's yours. You can do what you like with her. You'll get no argument from me," Ralph assured her, seeming a little surprised by her vehemence. "I look forward to meeting her," he paused and glanced ruefully at his plastered leg. "Though when that will be, I cannot say."

Abby flushed with embarrassment over her outburst. "It is I who should apologize, Mr. Ross," she forced herself to say. "After all, it was you who rescued her from that horrible man who was beating her. I suppose now she is mine, I feel rather protective of her."

Damian nodded. "I know exactly how you feel," he said, looking at her so strangely, she had to avert her eyes. *What did he mean by that, I wonder?*

"Changing the subject, Ralph," he suddenly said, "will you mind if I take a few days off to go to London? I have some business to do there. I'm going to dine with Lyle as well and catch up on news."

For some unfathomable reason, Abby's heart sank.

"Not at all, old chap. With the new horses coming, you're free to go and enjoy yourself for a while, blast you. I'd love to come with you, but there's no chance of that at present. Give my best regards to Lyle. Ask him to come and visit us sometime and see what he thinks of the setup."

Damian laughed. "Not much chance of that, I'm afraid. You know what he's like; he thrives on the fetid air of the great metropolis. But I'll pass on your regards. I'll be off sometime tomorrow if that's all right. I'll only be gone a few days."

"Perfectly fine, though I shall miss your company," Ralph admitted with a rueful smile. "I suppose I'll just have to put up with my sister's. Ah, poor me!"

"Poor me, rather," Abby retorted, making a face at him, in hopes of concealing the crushing disappointment she felt at the thought of Damian going anywhere for any length of time.

* * *

"It sounds to me like you've landed yourself in a pretty pickle, my friend," said Lord Lyle Bruton, Viscount Ismay, as he folded his long frame into the leather seat on the opposite side of the table to Damian, in a dim corner of Rafferty's Chop House in London's Cheapside.

"I warned you, this is the sort of thing that happens when you leave the safety of London and venture into the provinces," he went on with a shudder, simultaneously holding up two fingers to a waiter. "There's nowhere to hide out there and no friends to shield you from the dangers."

"Oh, do shut up, you nincompoop," Damian rebuked him mildly. "You do talk a lot of rot."

Lyle grinned. "That's why you missed me so much, you just had to rush back and see me, even though you've hardly been gone two weeks. Two weeks! And look at the trouble you're in already. It serves you right for deserting me. Admit it, you need me, my dear fellow."

Damian had to laugh. "I suppose I must do," he agreed, welcoming the delivery of a tankard of ale from the waiter.

"Thank you, my good man," Lyle said, as the waiter set his drink down on the table. "Two steak and oyster pies, with all the trimmings, quick as you like," he added with an imperious wave, sending the waiter scuttling off. Both men drank deeply of the ale and sat back, making satisfied noises as they wiped the foam from their lips.

Lyle set down his tankard and leaned his elbows on the table, his warm, hazel eyes fixing on Damian. "Now, tell me more about this mysterious lady who has caught your eye. Now, that is a sentence I never thought I'd hear myself say. Good Lord! Damian Ross, beguiled by some elderly enchantress who's buried herself in the depths of Buckinghamshire? Am I having a nightmare?" He chortled at his own wit and pinched himself theatrically.

"She's not elderly, she's twenty-six," Damian corrected him.

"You called her an old maid," Lyle protested.

"I said she acts like an old maid. She's young and ravishingly beautiful, but she never leaves the country."

"As I said, it sounds fishy. If she's as ravishing as you say, then she ought to be married by now. What's wrong with her?"

"That's what I like about you, Lyle, your incisive mind, the way you cut though all the palaver and straight to the crux of the matter."

"Oh, do stop with the flattery and answer the question."

"There's nothing at all wrong with her that I can make out, except that she despises me. Other than that, she's perfect in every way."

"No insanity in the family?"

"She's Ralph's sister, for goodness' sake!"

"Oh yes, so you said. Well, he's a stand-up fellow. But sisters, hmm, I have two, and they're a different kettle of fish altogether, like high-strung fillies. A chap's sister is no reflection on him, as I know to my cost," he declared, a small frown passing fleetingly across his broad brow.

"Good Lord! I'm in sore need of good advice," Damian complained, leaning back in his chair as the plates of steaming steak and oyster pie arrived on the table. "Why on earth did I think of asking you?"

Chapter Fourteen

"You thought of me because you know I always have your best interests at heart," Lyle said, picking up his silverware and attacking the food enthusiastically.

"So you say, but I'm beginning to doubt it," Damian said, also starting to eat.

"Unfair!" Lyle countered. "What is it you want to hear?"

"I want your honest opinion on what I should do."

Lyle swallowed a mouthful of dinner, then waved his fork at Damian and said, "But why? You know what I'm going to tell you. You, who has for many years publicly sworn to remain a bachelor unto death. So, you have met a pretty lass in the country. What of it? Are you seriously going to throw away your principles over her? I think not."

"There's no question of that at all," Damian retorted, suspecting he was lying. "I'm a man of principle, and you can rely on that. It's just that ..." He trailed off, his fork poised over his plate as he groped for the right words.

"Yes?"

"It's just that, well, she has a strange effect on me, Lyle. When I first saw her—I didn't know who she was then, mind you—she was racing across a hill on horseback, silhouetted against the sky. And Lyle, she was riding astride!" He paused as the scene replayed in his mind, and a shiver of his original excitement ran up his spine.

Lyle eyes widened. "Was she, by Jove?! Now, that's a bit of a corker all right."

"Exactly. It was like a vision sent from heaven tailored just for me. A beautiful horse, a beautiful rider in a crimson dress, riding like a man. Well, it fair took my breath away."

"I can imagine."

"And then, I found out she's Ralph's sister. And she's even more gorgeous to look at close up."

Lyle scoffed. "Come on, Damian, get a grip. How many gorgeous women are there in London? Tons of them. She cannot be that special. And you said she despises you anyway, so what's the problem?" He sawed a piece of beef in half, slathered it with gravy, and popped it in his mouth.

"I know very well how many beautiful women there are in London. I've been evading many of them for years," Damian responded. "Not a single one of them has had the same effect on me as Abby Lucas, and I want to know why."

Lyle finished his mouthful of beef and took a thoughtful slurp of ale before replying. "Well, it's obvious, isn't it? She's the one. The one who will finally ensnare you and drag you up the aisle. Before you can turn around, you'll find yourself shackled for life. This is a very dangerous situation, Damian, I jest not. If you ask me, it's lucky she despises you, but that could change at any moment. Get out of there before it's too late is my advice."

"But how can I? You know I've only just gone into partnership with Ralph. I can hardly let him down now, even if I wanted to. Which I don't. With things as they are between me and the old man, I need to make a go of this venture and prove to him I don't need his money or the title."

Lyle threw down his silverware and shook his head at Damian, looking appalled. "This is bad, worse than I thought. I'm going to have to buy a new suit for your wedding, aren't I? I can see it coming. All my friends are getting picked off like fish in a barrel. I thought at least I could rely on old Damian to remain true to the brotherhood, but I see I was wrong. This is a black day, Damian, a black day indeed."

"There you go again, you driveling fool. Honestly, you should be on the stage. I have not changed my views on matrimony one iota, so stop making such a fuss about it. I have no intention of getting married, not to her or anyone else."

"I'm relieved to hear it, old chap," Lyle said, sufficiently mollified to go back to his dinner.

"But I want you to find why she's so reclusive. Apparently, she's stayed in the country for the last four years, hasn't attended the Season, never comes to town, and has a low opinion of the *Ton*."

"Can't blame her for that," Lyle interjected.

"But she's young and beautiful and clever and funny, so why has she turned herself into a recluse? Why is she not married? She has a secret, I'm sure if it, and it's driving me mad not knowing what it is. I have a feeling it's the key to the way she is, why she treats me so coldly. Something happened four years ago, and I need to know what it was."

"Why four years ago?" Lyle repeated.

Damian filled him in on the two women at the horse fair, what they had said, and how Abby had reacted.

"That is curious," Lyle mused when he had finished. "Perhaps there's some sort of scandal attached to her. Clearly, from what you say, she was unfortunate enough to be the subject of talk. I can find out about her past for you quite easily, I'm sure. But when I do, what are you going to do with the information?" he asked suspiciously.

"How can I answer that, you dunderhead, when I don't know what it is yet? Ask me when you find out. But whatever it is, it certainly won't involve marriage!" Damian was so excited by the time he finished speaking, he had to take a long drink of ale to calm himself down.

"Hmm, it certainly is odd that she's still single if she's as lovely as you say," Lyle murmured.

"I cannot put into words how attractive she is."

"You're scaring me again, old chap."

"I can't help that. I need to know what makes her tick, and if there is something wrong with her, then I need to know that too."

"Have you thought of asking her?"

"Have you ever been stabbed with a dinner fork?"

"I say, steady on. What about Ralph? Couldn't you get it out of him somehow?"

"He adores her, and he's very protective of her. All he'll say is that she's shy and doesn't like strangers. Me being the stranger in question."

Lyle nodded. "All right, I'll make a few subtle enquiries and see what I can turn up. I'll drop you a line as soon as I know something."

"Thank you, Lyle. I owe you a favor."

"The biggest favor you can do me is to promise never to send me an invitation to your wedding."

"I can promise you that, certainly," Damian replied, feeling quite sure at that moment that he was not lying, either to Lyle or to himself.

* * *

"I feel I am quite ridiculous, Claire," Abby said to her friend as they sat sharing a pot of tea in the front room of Worsley vicarage. She sighed with exasperation, "How can I possibly miss him? It simply does not make sense."

"I disagree. If you allowed yourself to put aside your fears and think about things logically, it makes perfect sense," Claire replied with perfect equanimity.

Abby frowned. "What do you mean?"

"Abby, you already know what I mean. You have told me so yourself. You were fearful of Mr. Ross initially because he was a stranger. You are wary of strangers for reasons we both know."

"Yes."

"You resented him as well because Ralph went into partnership with him and not you."

"Yes."

"But your logical mind knows that it was not his fault, and the more you get to know him, the more you find yourself liking him."

"Yes, that is it in a nutshell. With everything he does, he makes it harder and harder for me to disklike him."

"Then, let us agree, you do like him."

"But that is neither here nor there, Claire. I do not *want* to like him. His very presence at Worsley, occupying the position I planned for myself, means I should not like him. He ought to mean nothing to me. And I certainly should not be missing him."

"Explain to me a little more about what you mean when you say you miss him."

"Oh, this is so embarrassing. Well, when I'm at the stables or out riding, I find myself thinking about him and wishing he were there too."

"Go on," Claire encouraged, listening intently.

"I keep finding myself dangling about by the front windows of the house, staring down the drive, straining my eyes to see if he is coming back." She spoke with an increasing sense of bewilderment. "And when Ralph and I eat dinner, I keep looking over at his empty seat and feel a strange sort of hollow in my heart and lose my appetite. In short, I am mooning about like a schoolgirl with a crush. And it is intolerable!"

"Good grief. All that, even though you say you seldom speak to him?" Claire asked, her big brown eyes filled with concern behind her spectacles.

"Yes." Abby nodded. "Which makes it even more nonsensical that I should feel like this. Oh, what is wrong with me, Claire?!"

"I am not sure, but Abby, my dear, do you think there might be a chance you are falling in love with Mr. Ross?"

Abby's hand shook so violently at the shocking suggestion, her teacup rattled loudly in its saucer. Fearing a breakage, she hurriedly placed them on the table and turned to stare at her friend.

"In love?" she echoed, aghast. "With Damian Ross? Are you mad?"

"Possibly. But look at what you have told me. You say you become flustered in his presence, you feel the lack of his company when out riding and at dinner, you look constantly for his return. Are these not the classic signs of a *tendresse*?"

Abby felt hot all over, and her heart began racing. "No, that is impossible."

"Is it? I would say you are pining for Mr. Ross," Claire said with sympathy.

Holding down her panic, Abby shook her head in vehement denial. "No, it cannot be so. It is something else. I am merely reacting to his unsettling presence in my life. Or I am coming down with something."

Yes, that must be it," she gabbled, feeling as though she were drowning and grasping at straws.

"Oh, Abby, can you hear yourself? Have you not already admitted how much you secretly admire him and also complained how hard it has become to keep him at arm's length?"

"Yes, I have, but you are wrong, Claire. I have never been in love, but I am certain that *liking* someone is very different from *loving* them. I admit I *like* Damian. However, I think I would know if I was in love with him." She spoke with a confidence she did not feel at all.

"Are you sure? Because after all you have told me, I fear you may be lying to yourself. It seems to me that you have developed feelings for Mr. Ross. You may not like it, but you can do yourself no good by denying it."

Almost overwhelmed by the storm conflicting emotions raging inside her, Abby put her head in her hands and moaned, "I am not in love with Damian Ross. I absolutely am not in love with him. I cannot be!"

But what if Claire is right? What she says makes sense. I did get jealous at the thought of him being pursued by other ladies, and perhaps I am pining for him. Oh, Lord, please do not let me be in love with him!

"I feel we are going around in circles," Claire said, breaking into Abby's thoughts. "You are no better off than when you first came in. I do not know how to advise you. But I feel I must ask you, Abby, is it possible that Mr. Ross could share your feelings?"

"What?!" Abby exclaimed, sitting bold upright, as shocked by Claire's question as she had been by Maude's suggestion that Damian looked at her admiringly. In her mind, the answer was obvious.

"No, of course not. One might as well expect snow in June. Besides, Maude has already pointed out to me what a catch he is and how he likely has hordes of beautiful and charming ladies chasing after him. And, oh—" She broke off in sudden dismay.

"What is it?" Claire's brows rose inquiringly.

"When she said that, about beautiful, charming ladies, I felt ... jealous," Abby admitted in a whisper, feeling as guilty as if she had just confessed to a murder.

Claire's expression turned grave. "Oh, dear. That is serious indeed, Abby. Why should you feel jealous if you do not—"

Abby cut her off. "I am not in love with him, I tell you!" she declared, her stomach tying itself in knots as the alarming possibility pressed down on her.

Claire held up a placating hand. "Very well, Abby. But look here, I know you will not agree with me, but the fact is, you are beautiful and charming yourself. To my mind, Mr. Ross would be a fool if he did not admire you."

Abby brushed off her words. "I have told you, that is as likely as snow in June. And even if it were so, which I am certain it is not, it would make no difference."

"Whyever not?" Claire asked with a puzzled frown. "Surely, if you both liked each other, all would be well."

"No, it would not, not at all. Let us pretend he is passionately in love with me. How long do you think that would last once he sees how disfigured I am?"

"I know you fear he will reject you on those grounds, but—"

"There is no 'but,' Claire. It is a certainty."

"Abby, unless you can read his mind, you cannot be certain," Claire insisted. "You are assuming it, that is all. The truth is, instead of taking a chance on the possibility of a friendship, or perhaps even greater happiness, by letting him make up his own mind, you have decided for him."

Abby's heart ached as familiar feelings of loss and sorrow mingled with regret when a fleeting vision of a happy future as Damian's wife, the mother of his children, flickered through her mind.

But it went out like a snuffed candle, to be replaced by another that filled her with anguish—of Damian's beautiful green eyes filled with repulsion when he finally beheld her ugly scars.

Chapter Fifteen

"I wish things were different, Claire, believe me," Abby finally said in a choked voice she hardly recognized as her own. "No one could wish it more than I."

Once again, her friend placed a comforting hand on hers. "Abby, I beg you, please do not throw this possible chance of happiness away through fear of what you imagine might happen. Give Mr. Ross the benefit of the doubt and let him decide for himself. If he turns out to be the sort of man who is so superficial as to care about a few scars, then he is not worthy of your love, and the pain you feel will soon pass. Be brave and take a chance," she urged gently.

Her emotions in turmoil, Abby shook her head. She squeezed Claire's hand, then let it go. "I cannot, Claire, I simply cannot."

* * *

When she left the vicarage a short while later, she did not feel ready to go home. Instead, she turned Silver into the meadows and then rode up into the hills, hoping to find in nature's tranquil beauty some sort of respite from her torment.

But she only found herself crying, the tears cold on her cheeks as she sped along the ridge on Silver's back with Claire's words echoing in her ears over and over.

What on earth am I crying about? she chided herself, dashing the tears away with the back of her hand.

She had gone to Claire hoping for comfort, for clarity. It was not her friend's fault that she had come away with neither of those things. She could not explain to Claire that she had plunged back into the dark despair she had so painstakingly hauled herself out of in the months and years following the fire.

But this time, it felt even more crushing.

* * *

That evening, when she and Ralph were dining alone for the fourth night in a row, as always, she tried to put a cheerful face on for his benefit. She even made herself eat all of her dinner, though she did not feel like eating. But he must have sensed something was wrong, because between the main course and pudding, he asked her about it.

"What's up, Little Sister? Something's on your mind, I can tell. Care to tell old Ralph what it is? Maybe I can help?" He smiled at her kindly, the corners of his blue eyes crinkling deceptively, for his gaze was searching.

"I am perfectly all right. Why do you ask?" She was immediately on guard, cursing his perceptiveness and hating herself for keeping things from him. It was not something she would normally choose to do. But when it came to her feelings about his friend and partner, there was so much at stake for him if anything went wrong, she felt forced to.

"Oh, nothing in particular," he replied with a shrug. "You have just seemed rather subdued these past few days. Are you still upset with me for making you attend the horse fair, is that it? You are holding a grudge because I winkled you out of your shell and made you venture out in public, perhaps?"

"No, of course not. I have forgiven you for that."

"Ah, then it must be because of Damian," he said, sending her heart rate soaring. *How can he know that? Am I so easy to read?*

"Damian? Whatever do you mean?" She awaited his response with bated breath.

"For bringing him here, you know, making you share the place with a stranger, taking him on as my partner and all that."

Relief washed over her. "Well, I have not entirely forgiven you for that, I admit. You did spring it all on me, which you know I hate. But I suppose one can get used to anything if one has no choice."

He regarded her for a few moments, apparently unperturbed by her small dig. "I had no choice but to ask it of you, Abby, in the circumstances. And I want you to know how proud I am of you for doing so well. I know it must have taken a lot to go out in public at a crowded event like that. You were very brave. And you did not get ill or faint, did you?"

She toyed with the idea of telling him about Araminta and June and her "funny turn," but saw no point in worrying him. "No. I admit, I was very nervous, and I did not like the crowds at all. But I did enjoy the purchase of the horses, and I do have Alba to show for it, so it was not all bad. I am still alive."

"Quite so. You are still very much alive." He gave her a meaningful nod as he let the words sink in.

"I presume you are trying to say that because I survived the ordeal, you were right to have made me go and face my fears," she told him with a small smile.

He laughed like a boy caught out in a prank. "Spot on, Little Sis. But I was also very glad, not to say relieved, that you managed to work with Damian in selecting two very good horses without any fights breaking out."

"You sound as though you expected us to resort to fisticuffs and be arrested by the constables for a breach of the peace," she said, trying to sound light-hearted in order to deflect any further questions about what was on her mind.

He laughed again. "You can be very fierce at times, Abby, though perhaps you do not realize it. I was a little worried for Damian, I confess. You have not exactly been friendly towards him. I thought that if you two spent some time together, it might help to melt your permafrost."

She sat up in her chair, indignant. "You mean you threw us together like that deliberately?"

"No, it was necessary that you should both go, for reasons I do not need to explain again." He gestured at his leg. "But I also saw it as a good opportunity to foster a friendship between you."

"I hope you are not going to take me to task again about my reserve towards him, Ralph. I have been trying my best, you know," she replied defensively.

"I have no intention of taking you to task about anything, Sister dear. As far as you giving poor old Damian the cold shoulder, I've decided you'll thaw out in your own time, and he's big and ugly enough to look after himself.

"Talking of ugly, I'm no judge myself of a gentleman's attractions when it comes to the female point of view, but I have it on good authority that Mr. Ross is regarded as something of a looker among the ladies. Not many would choose to resist his charms, apparently. Why should you be any different in the end?" he teased.

A chill ran through her. "What a disgusting thing to say about your own sister. Sometimes, I really could disown you as my brother, Ralph."

"I know, darling, but isn't that what big brothers are for, upsetting their sisters and being generally annoying?" he joked, seeming pleased with himself. "Besides, you adore me and would never disown me in a million years."

"Hm, that is why you get your way far too often," she retorted with perfect seriousness.

"But joking aside, Abby, dear, as I said before, it would mean so much to me personally and to the future of the business if you and Damian could be friends. And the way you succeeded at the horse fair proves how well you work together. It is but a short step from that to friendship."

"Yes, all right. You need not go on about it," she answered defensively. "You started off asking me if I was all right, but it appears that was a subterfuge for you to again press me to be friends with Mr. Ross."

He snorted. "That is a perfect example of my point. Why do you insist on calling him Mr. Ross? It's ridiculous formality. He's asked you to call him Damian several times. To keep on refusing is bordering on unkindness, Abby."

"Ah, I was right. You are taking me to task again."

He sighed. "I did not intend to, and I do not wish to press you. But how do you think Damian feels about it? A chap does have feelings, you know."

Abby stared at him, dumbstruck. For the first time, she considered the possibility that she could be making Damian unhappy. The excruciating pain that lanced through her then was totally unexpected, and it shook her to her core. Shame and guilt swept in, mingling with the whirl of conflicting emotions already pulling her in different directions.

Oh, what if it is true and I am causing him pain when he has been nothing but patient and kind to me? He saved my life, and Alba's too. Ralph is right; he deserves better. Oh, what am I to do?!

She felt caught in a trap of her own design, and it was on the tip of her tongue then to tell Ralph the truth. But she stopped herself.

What should I say, then? How will he react if I tell him that there is every possibility I am falling for his friend and business partner, and whether or not Damian reciprocates that feeling—a slim possibility, I admit—I stand to have my heart broken all over again?

She was still considering telling him when Ralph spoke again, breaking into her gloomy reverie. And what he said sent all other thoughts flying from her mind and threw her into a fresh state of panic much worse than the last.

* * *

"A masked ball, eh? What do you think of that, Lady Abby? A splendid idea, is it not?" Damian asked, looking across Ralph's bed at Abby, who was sitting opposite him as the three of them played cards on the counterpane.

"Yes, splendid," she replied with a nod. Her smile was small, yet nevertheless warmed him like a summer's day.

However, he detected anxiety in her eyes and immediately understood that she found the idea of opening her home to a crowd of people, mostly strangers from the *Ton*, the very opposite of splendid.

Although he had not said it at the time, it was one of the reasons why, on his return from London the previous evening, when Ralph had first mentioned his plan to hold a ball to officially launch the business, he had immediately thought of Abby and made a suggestion.

"An excellent idea, my friend, but can we make it a masked ball? I do not want to be recognized as Viscount Amberley by anyone who might report my whereabouts back to the old man," he had said, determined his father should not track him down. "A masked ball would allow me to remain incognito."

Ralph had grinned and slapped his back. "Genius! It will add a whole new twist of intrigue to the proceedings. A masked ball it shall be!"

Called back to the present by Ralph exclaiming, "Hit!"—a request for another card in the game of vingt-et-un they were playing—Damian, as the dealer, skillfully flicked one to him. At the same time, he asked casually, "Do you have a date in mind for this social extravaganza, Ralph? And whom do you think we should invite?"

"I was thinking about the last Saturday in May. Or perhaps the first week in June," Ralph replied, intently inspecting his revitalized hand of cards, his neutral expression giving nothing away as to its value. "As to guests, I have some names in mind, but I thought you and I could put our heads together and come up with a few more. As long as they're horse mad and loaded with cash, they'll be welcome. It'll put us on the map as trainers nicely, even though we shan't have any runners of our own until next spring."

"Excellent. So, we have a couple of weeks to decide on our disguises, then. Where is the best place locally for that, do you think, Abby?" he asked, transferring his gaze to her.

She shifted uncomfortably in her chair, and his heart clenched as he half expected her to freeze him out again. But she met his eyes and said quite pleasantly, "I have not shopped there myself for some time, but I believe Fortescue's in Beaconsfield has a large selection of such items in stock. And if they do not have anything you like, they will order for you from their London store."

"Thank you for the tip. I shall pay them a visit very soon. Have you any thoughts about your own costume?"

Her lovely eyes flew wide. "Er, not really. I mean, not yet," she replied, the faintest blush tinting her cheeks, which he always found adorable.

"I think I shall go as some sort of horse," Ralph put in, "but I shall have to come up with a famous one that everyone will know."

"With your leg as it is, perhaps you could consider the wooden horse of Troy? That had wheels, did it not?" Damian suggested jokingly, referring to Ralph's recent announcement that he had ordered a bath chair, in order to be wheeled about the ballroom.

A sudden giggle from Abby drew his attention. Something warm glowed in his chest at the unexpected reaction. He caught her eye and smiled at her. And though she immediately lowered her eyes, a fanfare sounded in his brain. *At last, I have succeeded in making her laugh. This is progress indeed!*

Chapter Sixteen

While each of them examined the hand he had just dealt, Damian covertly watched Abby and mused on how much he had missed her whilst in London. Strangely, on the journey back to Worsley, with Lyle's warnings still ringing in his mind and certain he was not in danger because Abby was sure to greet his return with her usual frostiness, the hours could not seem to pass quickly enough for him.

He studied his cards sightlessly, while his mind went back to the previous evening.

He had been surprised by the way his heart had inexplicably lightened when the old manor came into view. When he alighted from the cab and glimpsed her pale, delicate features peeping out from behind the drapes, it had all but ignited in his chest.

Pull yourself together, man. She despises you and will be about as welcoming as an iceberg, so don't get excited, he had silently chided himself, striding inside the house, expecting her to have rushed off somewhere to avoid him.

He was startled, therefore, and came to a sudden halt when he found her standing before him, her small, delicate hands clasped demurely at her slender waist, a slight curve of her lips hinting at a smile.

How can she have grown even more beautiful in just a few days? he had silently asked himself in bewilderment, staring at her wordlessly, feeling as though he had just been punched in the chest. He had found himself waxing lyrical as he drank her in. *She is as radiant as the moon, her eyes have the same silvery hue, her skin is like alabaster, and her hair is the color of autumn leaves. And don't even get me started on her lips …*

"Shall I take your things, sir?"

"Eh? What?" It was the first time he had noticed the waiting maid. "Oh, yes, of course, thank you," he had muttered in confusion, handing over his hat, cane, gloves, and coat. She had placed them neatly on the stand by the door, then politely inquired if he wanted anything else.

"Um, no, er, thank you," he had said, dismissing her. With a brief curtsey, she had vanished below stairs, leaving him alone to face Abby.

"Good evening, Mr. Ross, I hope you had a pleasant journey," she had said with perfect civility if not exactly warmth.

Astonished that she should linger in his presence and actually deign to speak to him, he had been forced to gather his wits about him before finding his voice.

"Er, Lady Abby, I beg your pardon. You took me rather by surprise. A good evening to you as well." He had bowed respectfully and received a gracious nod in return. If he had not been mistaken, the corners of those perfect little rosebud lips had turned up a little further. With a jolt, his heart had begun racing. "The journey was tolerable, thank you. The rain held off. I trust you are well?"

Dashed silly small talk when there is so much I would like to say to her.

"I am, thank you. And yourself?"

"Yes, very well, thank you."

"Did you enjoy your stay in London? No doubt it made the country seem very dull."

"Not at all. I am glad to return to Worsley. I enjoyed the bustle of London when I was a younger man, but now it is far too busy for my liking. These days," he had added, once more admiring the beauty of her eyes, "I find there are far more attractions in the country."

"Oh, I agree," she had said, her fingers twisting into knots at her waist.

Silence had fallen and seemed to Damian to last a small eternity. He had groped for something to say. "Um, er, and how is your dear brother?"

The radiance of her sudden smile at the mention of Ralph had sent his pulse soaring.

"Well, in terms of personality, he is the same as always." Her little laugh had delighted his ears. "But as to his leg, it is the same as when you left. Healing slowly."

"Good, good. Splendid," he had murmured absently, hardly taking in the words because she was so mesmerizing.

The atmosphere had been electric, the air charged as if before a storm, as they stared at each other, separated by only a few feet. A sudden wave of heat had washed over Damian, but the next moment, he felt cold.

The hall clock had ticked and then tocked hollowly, marking the passing seconds in yet another pressing silence.

Again, he had fumbled for something to say. "Horses all right? How's Alba getting on? Any improvement there?"

Her face had lit up once more. "Oh, yes, she is much improved. You must come and see. She has been out in the paddock and is eating like the proverbial horse."

He had laughed, genuinely delighted by her wit and the fact she had shared a joke with him—a so far unheard-of occurrence. As was her invitation. "That is kind of you to ask me. I shall certainly go and see her."

By that time, the tension had been so great, he felt that if something did not give soon, he would explode.

"Have you dined?" she had asked at last, the radiance of her smile fading a little. But it had not disappeared.

"Er, no, but I had a bite to eat for luncheon at the inn at Southerwick."

"Then you must be hungry. I am afraid Ralph and I have had our dinner already, but I can have something hot brought up for you."

Her apparent concern for his comfort and wellbeing had been a stunning revelation that temporarily robbed him of speech. Eventually, he had managed to reply, "That would be nice, thank you. I am rather hungry. Actually, I was intending to go and see Ralph. Perhaps I could have my dinner with him, on a tray?"

"Yes, of course. He has been complaining of boredom and will be pleased to see you."

And you? he had wanted to ask. *Are you pleased to see me?*

She had given a little nod, unknotted her fingers, and pressed her hands together tightly. "Well, I shall see to the food and give you both a chance to catch up before joining you later for a hand or two of vingt-et-un."

"I look forward to it. Thank you again, Lady Abby."

"You are welcome, Mr. Ross." She had suddenly blushed and appeared flustered. "I mean to say … Damian."

Well, knock me down with a feather, why don't you? he had thought, his amazement growing. A thrill had shot through him to hear his given name on her lips, and he had been excited by its implications. *What on earth has happened to bring about this remarkable change in her in just a few days? I must go away more often.*

His elation had made him feel like seizing her about the waist and dancing her around the room in jubilation. *But unfortunately, that is out of the question. I must not scare her off by seeming over-excited or acting as if I have scored a point against her, not now that we seem to be getting somewhere.*

So, he had merely inclined his head and smiled to acknowledge her concession. "Thank you again, Lady Abby."

She had lowered her eyes and cleared her throat, clearly feeling awkward. Then, as if inwardly steeling herself, she had met his gaze once again, her eyes flashing like two newly-minted shillings in the dim light of the low-ceilinged hall.

"You had better call me Abby then, I suppose, if we are to be on first-name terms. If you do not mind, that is."

He had not been able to stop the grin that formed on his lips. "I shall be honored ... Abby," he had replied with a half bow, the name tripping off his tongue like a beautiful melody.

She had exhaled in obvious relief. "I am glad that is settled then. Now, if you will excuse me, I shall go and order some supper for you."

"I am grateful indeed. Abby." *Abby, Abby, Abby, beautiful Abby!*

She had turned away, the skirts of her pretty lilac gown swishing as she headed to the far door.

He had moved quickly with intention. "Do allow me to open the door for you," he had said, arriving there a split second before she did. Their hands had collided on the door handle. The familiar spark crackled between them. It had made him jump, and her too, because she had snatched her hand back, her eyes wide with ... *what, exactly?*

Every nerve ending in his body had stood on end.

"Thank you," she had murmured, giving him the pleasure of admiring her slender white neck at close quarters as she stepped past him into the passage beyond, trailing the scent of roses. He had breathed in the intoxicating fragrance as he watched her go, admiring her slender, graceful figure as she glided away.

For several long moments after she had disappeared, he had stood rooted to the spot, staring after her.

"Well, I never, that is a turn up for the books," he had mused under his breath, unable to stop grinning. It had been so very refreshing not to feel despised by the woman who had come to occupy so much of his waking thoughts as well as his dreams.

"I wonder what further conversational delights I have to look forward to now that civilized communication has been established and we are on first name terms, Abby," he had added in an undertone, finally closing the door and heading for the staircase.

He had been half way to Ralph's chambers when it occurred to him that Ralph might be responsible for Abby's turnaround. He had never complained to his friend about his sister's coldness, but he knew Ralph was aware of it, usually laughing it off as her "shyness."

But knowing Ralph's kind nature, it seemed entirely possible that out of concern for a friend's feelings, he would have spoken to her about it and asked her to mend her ways.

"That would be somewhat disappointing," Damian had muttered as he put his hand up to rap on Ralph's door. "How much sweeter it would be to know it was by her own volition ... because she can no longer hide the fact she actually likes me."

"Twenty-one!" Abby declared, her voice dragging him abruptly back to the present and Ralph's chamber. She laid down her cards on the coverlet, a ten, an eight, and a three.

Ralph groaned. "Blast you, Sister, you have the devil's luck!" he grumbled, tossing his own cards down contemptuously. "Twenty-eight. I blame the dealer," he added, glaring at Damian in mock accusation.

Damian laughed and showed his own hand. "Don't be such a bad looser, old chap. I'm no better off. Look, a measly sixteen," he told him. Then, looking at Abby, he added, "Well done again, Abby. You definitely have a knack for the game."

"How can one have a knack for a game that is based on pure chance, Damian? I have just been lucky with my cards this evening, that is all," she replied with a self-deprecating chuckle.

"Well, it is your turn to be dealer," he told her gathering up the cards, buoyed up by her friendly manner and feeling a little tingle each time she called him by name. The first time she had done it in Ralph's hearing, his friend had given him a sly wink when she was not looking, as if to say, "See, I told you she'd thaw out eventually." Damian had smiled back.

They finished another hand of the game, and then Ralph wanted some refreshment. "Claret, that is what I need," he declared. "I'm parched."

"Sir Henry says you are not supposed to drink and have your medicine," Abby warned.

"Then dash the medicine. Give me claret! I demand claret," he roared, playfully beating the counterpane with his fist.

So, claret was brought up along with a plate of sandwiches, and they all partook. Damian noticed that Abby hung back while he and Ralph discussed the arrangements for the forthcoming ball and felt a wave of sympathy for her. She said not one word to criticize or challenge her brother's plans. But it was obvious to him from her tentative show of enthusiasm that she was trying her best to hide her anxiety at the prospect of the forthcoming social invasion of her home by members of the *Ton*.

But what else can she do but go along with it when Ralph gives her no choice? he wondered as he waited for Abby to deal a new hand. He briefly looked for any sign of discord between the siblings but saw none. They seemed perfectly happy with each other. He could not work it out.

Ralph knows Abby will be even more terrified by the prospect of a ball here at Worsley than she was by attending the horse fair. He must know better than anyone the secret of why she's so afraid of strangers, yet it's almost as though he's deliberately using the business as a pretext to force her out of her shell and back into society.

Then it struck him. *I'll wager Ralph's worried sick about her future. Of course, any caring brother would want his sister to be happy, to have something more to look forward to than being a lonely old maid. Is this his way of trying to bring it about?*

Convinced he was right, his respect for Abby's courage in facing her fears for Ralph's sake grew. But so did his curiosity about what she was hiding about her past. Unfortunately, he had to hope Lyle would come through with that information soon. In the meantime, though he felt bad for Abby's distress, he could only approve of Ralph's intentions. He realized it must be very hard for Ralph to make her miserable, but he had clearly decided it would be better for Abby to suffer in the short term in order to ensure at least a chance of greater happiness in the future.

He wants her to marry!

The realization hit him like a flying cannonball smashing into the walls of a castle under siege, leaving him standing in the wreckage of his defenses, with one shining new resolve in mind that was profoundly shocking to him.

If anyone is going to marry Abby Lucas, then it's going to be me!

Chapter Seventeen

With this shattering revelation rapidly rearranging all his internal furniture, not to mention his entire world view, Damian sipped his claret and surreptitiously watched Abby over the rim of his glass.

"So, Abby, dear, I trust we can count on you to make all the necessary domestic arrangements for entertaining a large number of guests," Ralph said. "I intend to open up the ballroom for the occasion."

"I suppose if one is throwing a ball, then a ballroom is as good a place as any to hold it," she said drily, her expression growing more tense as her brother continued outlining his expectations.

"And the décor should be appropriately splendid. Likewise the catering, etcetera." Ralph waved a dismissive hand, as though he thought Abby would achieve all this with no more than a snap of her fingers. Damian supposed it was part of his plan to force his sister to re-engage with society.

"Some will be staying overnight, of course, and need accommodation."

"I am aware of that, Ralph, thank you," Abby replied shortly, shuffling the deck of cards and starting to deal. "Once I have the guest list and an idea of numbers, I shall know what to do."

"Have you ever thrown a ball before, Ralph?" Damian asked, picking up his cards.

"No, I've only ever attended them," his friend replied. "But it's only a glorified dance. It cannot be very hard."

"It is very hard indeed, my friend. There are many things to consider beforehand." He reeled off a long list that made Ralph's jaw drop as he listened. "And that is just for the guests," Damian continued, secretly gratified by Abby's widening smile.

"We must also decide on our masks and obtain them. One person cannot do it all, Ralph. You and I must also do our part in organizing things as well. I suggest we all put our heads together and make a list of the tasks and then divide them up. Withers and Mrs. O'Connor should be present as well."

"Dash it all, Damian, you make it sound like hard work," Ralph remarked, throwing down a card and adding, "Hit!"

"Entertaining sophisticated people who are always vying to outdo each other in the social stakes is hard work, Ralph. For some, like Lady Lambourne and Lady Lucinda Page, it is an all-consuming vocation."

Abby looked at him aghast. "I hope we do not have to compete with those ladies. Was it not Lady Lucinda who had the tiger on display at one of her balls?"

"It was. I saw the beast with my own eyes. It looked so sad, I had to stifle the urge to secretly open the cage and let it out so it could wreak its bloody revenge on its captors," Damian admitted.

"Oh, the poor thing. I am sure I would be exactly the same. It is quite wrong in my view to treat such majestic animals as sideshows to be gawped at."

"Then we are in perfect agreement, Abby," he replied. "But then, when it comes to the mistreatment of animals, we have already discovered that, have we not? With Alba, I mean?"

"Yes, we have, I suppose. At any rate, music, dancing, good company, and good food and drink should be sufficient to entertain our guests. The park will be at its best at that time, and I am sure they will find it pleasant enough," she said firmly, breaking their gaze and returning her attention to the game.

"We couldn't afford a tiger anyway. But we could always put a few of the horses in dinner suits and let them wander about the ballroom," Ralph suggested, tongue-in-cheek.

"We could hitch one of them up to your bathchair, Brother, and get it to pull you about. It would save the fag of having to push you," Abby retorted.

Always impressed by her sharp wit, Damian could not help snorting with laughter. "That makes for an interesting picture," he said. "Yes, I think we should do it, but rather than engage a noble horse for the job, I suggest we acquire an ass."

All three burst out laughing at that, and while he was laughing, Damian realized he was genuinely happy. He looked over at Abby, whose face was alight with mirth, and their eyes met. His heart thudded hard in his chest and then went soaring like a bird to encounter the unmistakable warmth in hers. Elation flowed through him.

I've done it at last. I've finally worn her down and made her like me!

A determination rose in him to press home his advantage.

This ball cannot come soon enough for me, he thought exultantly. *I am going to do everything in my power to ensure she enjoys the evening. I want to see her smiling and laughing. And dancing. Dancing with me.*

* * *

"Ah!" Damian smiled and closed his eyes as he leaned on the paddock fence and inhaled deeply of the clean morning air. He let out the breath, opened his lovely green eyes, and asked, "Is it not a beautiful morning, Abby?"

A skylark's liquid song pierced the surrounding tranquility as she raised her head from Alba's neck and looked at him as if seeing him for the first time. It would not do to let him know she had been watching him covertly from the moment he had stepped into the stable yard, nor how her heart had jolted when she laid eyes on him.

Her heart had gone skipping inside her chest when he stopped to pull on his leather gloves and cast about him as though looking for someone, part of her hoping it was her.

She had pretended not to notice when he caught sight of her, but she was secretly thrilled by his broad smile and continued to spy on him as he made a beeline for her, striding out on his long legs, hopping fences with impressive ease to reach her all the faster.

Abby's heart was racing with excitement. *Stay calm. Be friendly, just not too friendly. He cannot know how I feel about him,* she recited in her head. But it was all but useless, and she knew it. The sheer magnetism of his presence was growing increasingly impossible to resist with every step he took.

Now, here he was, leaning on the fence a few feet away, looking criminally handsome in a long duster coat and high-top boots, his dark hair stirring in the warm breeze.

A smile came unbidden to her lips as she faced him. Despite her best efforts, it refused to leave. "Oh, good morning, Damian. I did not see you there," she fibbed, trying to sound neutral. "Yes, it is a lovely day indeed."

"A perfect day for a ride. Have you already been out today?" he asked casually.

"Yes, but that does not mean I shall not go out again."

He said nothing but nodded as if in approval. At that point, Alba nickered and went straight to him. Abby watched entranced as he laughed with pleasure when the white mare rubbed her head against his and nibbled gently at his ears and hair, her way of expressing her affection.

Damian petted her in return, clearly enjoying himself. Abby melted to see the tenderness in his eyes when looked at Alba and caught herself wishing he would look at her that way, even though she knew it was wrong.

"It's nice to know you remember me, Alba," he told the horse, producing a couple of sugar lumps from his coat pocket and feeding them to the horse, who crunched them up enthusiastically.

"Of course, she remembers you. You saved her from a fate worse than death, and horses never forget such kindnesses," Abby said, stroking Alba's flanks. "You are her hero."

He chuckled. "She is looking so well. She's really put on weight, and her eyes are nice and bright now. You've done wonders with her, Abby."

Abby could not help blushing with pleasure. "Thank you. Actually, I tried the diet you recommended, so her improvement is as much down to you as to me."

"That is gratifying to know. Mind if I take a closer look at her?"

"Not at all. I'm sure she would love it."

With an effortless hop, he was over the fence and landed beside her. Feeling a strong urge to hug him, Abby quickly moved away a few feet. She stood watching him as he gently examined Alba from head to hooves, even her teeth, which turned out to be remarkably good.

"You know, I don't think she's much more than four or five," he said eventually, giving the mare a final slap on the neck.

"That's what I think too. Her condition was so poor, it was deceptive. She likes being around the other horses as well. Silver has taken quite a shine to her. I wonder if we might not have some light-coated foals at some point in the future," Abby ventured daringly.

His remarkable green eyes met hers, and there was something in them that made her feel almost dizzy. "That would be something, would it not?" he said, his voice low and thrilling. "Maybe we'll even get a racer out of her, who knows?"

"That is probably a little ambitious," Abby replied with a laugh. "But as you say, you never know."

"Her wounds are healing well," he remarked, inspecting the scabbed-over wounds from the cruel whipping.

"Yes, but it will be some weeks before I shall risk putting a saddle on her again. I intend to take things very slowly."

"Very wise. I confess, I'm impressed with her progress. You are doing a fine job," he said again, fondly patting Alba's back.

When Alba suddenly neighed and walked off, she could see Damian was a surprised as she was. They both turned to see where she was off to. Billy the stable lad, back at work after recovering from his illness, was leading Silver and Warrior into the paddock. Quinton followed with some of the other horses. Alba and Silver immediately joined up, nuzzling each other.

"It looks like true love," Damian said, giving Abby a look that made her melt. Thankfully, he then changed the subject. "Well, are you excited about this afternoon?" he asked. The two new colts they had purchased at the fair were due to arrive later that day.

"Very," Abby replied with genuine excitement. "I cannot wait for Ralph to see them. I hope they have a comfortable journey and will settle in well with the others. Are you really going to wheel him out here in his new bathchair to see them?"

"Naturally. I said I would, and I am a man of my word. Even if it kills me. Besides, it will be a good test for the ball."

At the mention of the ball, her spirits fell. "Yes, I suppose it will."

Damian looked at her with touching concern. "What is it, Abby? Have I said something to upset you? If I have, I apologize."

"No, of course not," she answered, feeling awkward. *What should I say?* "I confess I am a little worried about the ball. There is so much to organize, and I want everything to go smoothly."

"Spoken like a true hostess," he replied, nodding sagely. "It's normal to be anxious about such things when one cares for one's guests, I think. My mother was always a bag of nerves whenever she threw an entertainment, but it always turned out to be a success in the end, so her worry was needless."

"Oh? Thank you, that is encouraging," she said untruthfully, nevertheless startled by the mention of his mother and moved by the hint of sadness in his voice. *So, he has lost his mother too,* she thought, feeling a connection with him. Clearly, his life had not been free of pain either. Moreover, it was the first time he had ever mentioned his family, and she was instantly curious to know more as well as acknowledge his kindness.

She chose her words carefully. "You speak as though she is no longer with us. If that is so, then I am very sorry to hear it."

He sighed. "She died almost ten years ago of a fever, when I was nineteen." He suddenly looked and sounded so bereft, Abby's heart softened further towards him. Nevertheless, part of her brain registered that he was twenty-nine. Somehow, it seemed the perfect age for a gentleman.

"I really am very sorry, Damian. You obviously cared for her very much."

"We were very close, yes. It was a great blow to me. I still think of her often and miss her support."

"Of course. I still miss our parents as well. Please accept my deepest sympathy for your loss," she told him, meaning every word.

"Thank you, Abby, that is kind." He paused for a moment as their gazes held. Once again, she had the weird sensation of the world telescoping down to just the two of them, and electrifying tingles raced over her skin.

He was the first to break the spell, seeming to shake off his sadness. He smiled at her warmly, his eyes crinkling attractively at the corners.

"Now, what was I saying? I forget. Oh, yes, about the ball. If I may give you a piece of unsolicited advice, I would suggest trying not to let your concern for your guests spoil your own enjoyment of the occasion. Much has already been accomplished. All the essentials for the décor have been ordered, the musicians are booked, the invitations are almost ready to send out—"

"Mrs. O'Connor is baking non-stop, and the ballroom has been dusted and polished to within an inch of its life," Abby chimed in, trying to sound light-hearted. "I appreciate and take note of your kind advice," she added, forcing a smile.

She was caught off guard when he almost seemed to read her thoughts. "I'm always in two minds about these things," he said confidingly. "Neither of us is very comfortable in a crowd, are we? That is part of the reason why I suggested making it a masked ball. I know I shall find it easier to deal with the influx of people if I'm in disguise."

"Yes, perhaps it will," she admitted, once again touched by his efforts to soothe her worries and surprised by his perceptiveness. She almost wished she could tell him how the thought of all those strangers coming into her house was growing more frightening with every passing day. But since that was impossible, she swallowed the impulse.

"Well, the new horses won't be here for hours. Shall we go for a ride?" he asked, giving her a hopeful look.

Flustered, Abby hesitated, torn in two directions. *You know you want to go with him, so go! What harm can an innocent ride do?* whispered the voice of her heart.

But another, the voice of reason, tried to drown it out. *Don't be a fool. Going with him will be a big mistake. You will only get hurt!*

One look into his beautiful green eyes, so full of hope and kindness, and her heart won out.

"All right," she heard herself say. "That would be very pleasant."

Chapter Eighteen

Within a quarter of an hour, they were cantering across the meadows towards the hills, Damian on Warrior and Abby riding Jasper, a black-coated, six-year-old gelding who loved a good run. Michael the stable lad, unwittingly doing double duty as chaperone, brought up the rear on Whisper, one of a matching pair of bay carriage horses, keeping a discreet distance.

Exhilarated as always by the speed and the warm breeze blowing on her face, Abby found herself laughing. When she exchanged looks with Damian, she saw he was doing the same, which made her laugh even more. It was simply glorious riding alongside him, knowing he was feeling the same joyous sense of freedom as she was.

When they came to the top of the hill and reined in, panting and flushed, she looked along the gallops stretching away into the distance and had a daring idea.

"Shall we have a race?" she asked him, her competitive spirit rising to the fore.

He laughed. "If you wish. But I warn you, be prepared to lose."

She tossed her head. "Oh, you are so certain of winning, are you?"

He slapped Warrior's neck. "On this one? Yes, I'm certain of it. Jasper's a fine horse, but Warrior is bigger and more powerful."

"Maybe so. Let's race and find out, shall we?"

Abby knew she was good horsewoman, and though he was undoubtedly right about Warrior being more powerful than Jasper, she was determined to put up a good show, even if she lost. "Shall we race to the burnt elm?" She pointed along the gallops to where the broken, blackened fingers of an elm blasted by lightning raked the sky about half a mile away, just beyond the fence.

He nodded. "All right. Michael can count us down."

Abby's stomach tightened with excitement as they leveled up their horses.

"On three. One, two, three!" Michael cried obligingly, apparently equal parts amused and perplexed by the antics of his betters.

On three, Abby was off, kicking up Jasper into a flying start. Beside her, Damian leaped away, the muscles in Warrior's powerful flanks rippling as he powered ahead. Keeping low in the saddle, Abby urged Jasper to go faster, the beast's hooves thundering across the turf as they flew over the ground towards the tree.

Damian, having the advantage, soon took the lead, his laughter trailing after him. But Abby was not dismayed. To be racing was enough in itself. She felt truly alive, all her worries snatched away by the breeze along with her own joyful laughter.

Beneath her, she could feel Jasper enjoying it too, the pair of them working in harmony to close the gap between them and their competitors.

Of course, Damian reached the tree first. But it was only a few seconds later that she reined Jasper in next to him. The horses panted and snorted happily as they jostled and danced about each other.

"A brave effort, Jasper, my friend," Abby murmured, unable to stop smiling as she scratched the horse's ears in thanks.

"I told you we would win," Damian said, looking heart-stoppingly handsome with his face flushed, hair blown back, a triumphant grin on his face.

"Yes, but only because Warrior is more powerful. You said so yourself," she replied, a little shocked by the teasing note in her voice. It bordered on flirtatious, and she had never flirted with anyone in her life!

She tried to rein in her excitement, saying, "Jasper did a grand job. A sugar lump and extra oats for you at dinner today, Jasper, my fine lad," she told him. Jasper nickered with pleasure as she petted his neck.

"You're an excellent horsewoman, Abby, but I had no idea how competitive you can be," Damian observed, eyeing her with a mixture of curiosity and, flatteringly, admiration.

"Is that a compliment or a rebuke?" she asked laughingly.

"I'm not sure yet. When I've decided, I'll let you know."

Before she could stop herself, she shot back in that same flirtatious way as before, "I look forward to finding out."

* * *

Later that afternoon, after enjoying the entertaining spectacle of Ralph being carried down the stairs by two burly footmen and placed in what he called his "new-fangled contraption," Damian was as good as his word and wheeled his friend out to the stables in his bathchair.

Abby walked alongside them, the excitement of the new horses' arrival temporarily eclipsing her overarching fear of the upcoming ball.

The transport wagon had already been sighted, and a lad had been dispatched to guide it up the rear driveway of the estate, where it came creaking on at a snail's pace, stretching Abby's patience. Finally, it pulled up in the stable yard, and they all eagerly gathered around.

"This is truly a momentous day," Ralph declared. "The real start of our adventure." He gestured at the wagon. "The seeds of greatness lie within."

"I admit, I have a tear in my eye," Damian confessed, smiling at Abby as he dashed it away with the back of his hand. She was touched by his show of emotion.

Quinton and Michael waited by the rear of the wagon for the door to be lowered. Abby held her breath. The door lowered, forming a ramp for the horses to descend. From inside, there was a rustling of straw, some whinnies and snorts, softly spoken words.

"Oh, look, here comes the first one," Abby cried, pressing her hands together in almost childish glee as the first of the colts came clattering down the ramp, led by a groom. It was the chestnut thoroughbred, Flame.

He came from a line sired by the famous Byerley Turk, one of three Arabian horses from which all European thoroughbreds were descended, and was once owned by the king of France. He pranced off the ramp onto the cobbles with a snort and an aristocratic flick of his mane, his flanks shiny as a new penny.

"Oh, is he not splendid?!" Abby cried, exchanging an excited glance with Damian.

"Even better than when we first saw him, I'll wager," he agreed, enthusiasm lighting up his handsome features.

"Now, that's a fine bit of bloodstock, all right," Ralph remarked admiringly, glowing with pleasure and pride as Michael walked the horse about, letting Flame stretch his long legs after the journey. "Never thought I'd own a beast like that. What a beauty." It warmed Abby's heart to see him so happy.

"Er, you only own half of him, old son. The other half is mine," Damian pointed out drily, making Abby giggle.

"Which half is whose, I wonder?" she joked.

"Depends which way we slice him, I suppose," Ralph said with a chuckle.

"Look, here comes the Arab, Spirit," Damian said, pulling their attention back to the wagon.

The Arabian gray came out more sedately, high-stepping down the ramp, head held high, and looking at them haughtily down his noble nose as if to say, "Look on my perfection, minions, and marvel."

Spirit's lineage was equally impressive as Flame's, for he was descended from the Godolphin Arabian, another of the three foundation sires, along with the Darley Arabian, all imported from abroad in the eighteenth century.

"He is very grand. He reminds me of a Sultan who expects awe and obeisance as his due," Abby said delightedly, signaling Quinton to walk the horses over for Ralph to look at more closely. Secretly, she wanted to save Damian from pushing the bathchair.

Ralph let out a low whistle as he stroked the proud Arabian's neck. "You can see the quality of his lineage, eh? He's going to make us famous and rich."

Flame stood quietly while Abby petted his neck. She whispered admiring words in his ear and slipped a sugar lump from her pocket to feed him. "He may be aristocratic, but he is not beyond crunching on a sugar lump like the humblest of hacks," she said, giggling when Flame nickered and nuzzled her ears with his velvety lips.

Damian was looking Spirit over, keeping a steadying hand on the horse's neck as it shifted restlessly. "He's tired of being shut up," Damian observed. "He wants to get out and run." Abby had to smile when she noticed him slipping the magnificent creature a sugary treat as well. Spirit eagerly whiffled it up from his hand, crunched it, and instantly calmed.

Ralph reached into his pockets and drew an apple from each one. He clicked his tongue, and the horses soon came to him, contentedly munching on the gift.

"Bribery. Works every time," Damian commented, making Abby chuckle.

They stayed and watched as the colts were released into the paddock. While Ralph looked on from his bathchair, peering at them through Damian's spyglass, Abby and Damian leaned on the fence a few feet apart. Despite the distance, her skin tingled at his proximity.

At the same time, she was struck by how right it felt to be there with him, watching the horses they had chosen together. *But that is the danger of him*, she reminded herself, feeling like a wild horse gradually being tamed against its instincts.

The other horses were already out in the neighboring field and had formed a knot by the fence between, clearly curious to meet the new arrivals. Everyone was interested to see how they would get on.

The colts circled the paddock a few times at a canter, kicking up their heels, obviously glad to be out of the wagon and back in the fresh air, on soft grass. Within minutes, they slowly gravitated towards the others.

Pretty soon, everyone was smiling and laughing in relief to hear the excited squeals and nickers coming from the horses as they greeted each other. There was a lot of nose touching, pawing at the ground, tails swishing, and prancing.

"This is very encouraging," Ralph observed, beaming at Abby and Damian. "I've said it before, but now I'm convinced of it. You two make a strong team when it comes to picking horses. I think maybe you should be in charge of that side of things from now on. Well done, the both of you."

"What an excellent idea," Damian said, smiling warmly at Abby. "What do you think, Abby?"

Abby hesitated, secretly thrilled by Ralph's proposal yet knowing how dangerous it was to feel like that. *What should I say? They are both looking at me so expectantly.*

In the end, she settled for a non-committal nod, saying, "I am glad you are so pleased with the horses, Brother. But the hard work of training the colts begins now. I think you should focus on that for the time being."

"Sensible words," Damian said, nodding his agreement.

Oh, Lord! Abby thought, feeling her defenses crumbling by the second. *Why does he have to be so perfect?!*

* * *

Damian experienced an extraordinary sense of wellbeing as he wheeled Ralph back towards the house in his bathchair, with Abby strolling alongside.

The arrival of the colts could not have gone better, and he was buoyed up by success. Success that was down to working together with Abby. Standing with her at the fence, watching the colts they had selected frolicking so happily with the other horses, had imbued him with a pleasurable warmth and sense of satisfaction he had never felt before. It was rather an epiphany. He could never have envisioned feeling such closeness, such natural accord, with a woman.

But Abby Lucas is not just any woman, is she? She's a precious, hidden gem.

Perverse as it was, there was a part of him that was glad she was so reclusive. It meant there was no competition to worry about. Because he knew it in his bones now: Abby was changing him. Things were getting serious. He was questioning his whole worldview on romantic entanglement. Even on, yes, he dared to admit it to himself, marriage.

He was enjoying himself so much, he did not notice the uneven edge of the flagstone ahead. The wheel of the bathchair butted hard against it, bringing it to a jarring halt.

"Ow! Careful, old son, that was painful!" Ralph complained with a grimace.

"Sorry, I didn't see the obstruction. Are you all right?" Damain asked contritely.

"I expect I'll live, but do pay attention in future. I don't fancy another six weeks stuck in this thing because you can't pay attention to where you're going," Ralph ribbed him, quickly regaining his good humor.

"That is very harsh, Brother," Abby chimed in. "Considering that Damian has hurt himself wheeling you about, you ought to be more grateful."

"Have I?" Damian asked, looking down, surprised to see blood pouring from a deep gash on the back of his hand where something sharp had torn through his glove. "Oh, so I have. I must have scraped it on the handle. 'Tis but a scratch," he added, pulling out a handkerchief and wrapping it around the wound.

"That needs cleaning at once before it gets infected," Abby declared. "Come with me, Damian. Ralph, wait there. I will send a footman back to fetch you."

The two men exchanged glances, brows raised. Damian found himself obediently following Abby inside.

"I'll just wait here, shall I? I mean, it's not as if I can go anywhere," Ralph called after them. When Damian glanced back over his shoulder. Ralph was grinning, and he wondered why.

Within ten minutes, he was sitting in a small back parlor, waves of pleasure rolling over him as Abby removed his ruined glove, rolled back his sleeve, and, with gentle fingers, inspected the wound on his hand.

As soon as they came in, she had ordered hot water, clean cloths, salve, and bandages to be fetched. A young maid was now in attendance, with the items laid out on the table.

"I assure you," he protested weakly as matter of form, "it's only a scratch. I can see to it myself."

"Nonsense. I insist on tending to it for you. It is a very nasty gash," Abby replied, the tips of her ears a delightful pink as she bent over his hand. She dabbed with exquisite delicacy at the wound with a moistened cloth, her touch light, intoxicating.

"And it is deeper than it looks." She flicked a glance at him with her silvery eyes. "Let me know if I am hurting you."

"You are being very gentle," he murmured, mesmerized by her look, her touch. He was sure he would not have minded staying there forever. Any discomfort he might have felt was trumped by the thrill of being so close to her.

Despite the presence of the maid, he felt tension crackling in the air between them.

As Abby worked diligently to clean the wound, he breathed in her rose perfume and silently marveled at the sheen on her rich, auburn hair, admiring the way it curled so adorably around her perfect little ears. It took all his self control not to reach out and touch it.

By the time she gently applied some salve, then lifted his hand to bandage it neatly, he was feeling almost drunk, as if on some particularly heady wine.

Would that I were more badly injured, he thought. *It would be worth it if I could only have her as my nurse.*

"There we are," she pronounced, regarding her handiwork approvingly. "Hopefully, there will be no infection since we caught it early." She wiped her hands on a cloth, her eyes meeting his. "Is that comfortable? It is not too tight, is it?"

"It's perfect, thank you. A very neat job."

Her smile was like the dawn. "Good. We cannot have you being laid low as well as Ralph."

"No, indeed," he said, reluctantly rising now the job was done, finding himself loath to leave her side.

While the maid gathered the debris, they looked at each other for a moment longer, the tension rising. When her cheeks had reached a pleasing shade of crimson, she cleared her throat and said, "Well, um, shall we join Ralph for tea?"

Do we have to? I would much rather stay here with you. "Yes, of course. Thank you again for your kind help."

He held the door open for her, his body tingling as she passed him by, following after her like a dog on a silken lead.

Chapter Nineteen

The day of the ball inevitably arrived. The late afternoon sun slanted through the high windows of Abby's chambers, turning the dust motes floating in the air to gold as she sat at her vanity, staring at her reflection with a mixture of stomach-roiling apprehension and disbelief.

Fingers knotted nervously in her lap, she watched as Maude fastened the final pearl comb into the curls atop her head, then artfully arranged long ringlets over her shoulder, concealing her scars.

"There," she pronounced, stepping back with a satisfied nod. "You're a vision, Milady."

"Thank you, Maude. I hardly recognize myself," Abby murmured, wondering if the stunning, sophisticated woman looking back at her from the mirror could really be her.

Her gown—a deep emerald-green silk trimmed in silver—fitted like a dream. The color made her eyes look brighter, her skin warmer, and set off her auburn hair perfectly. The neckline was modest but flattering, and the sleeves had just enough lace to cover her scars and feel elegant without being fussy.

The string of pearls resting on her collarbone matched her earrings. The set was a family heirloom last worn by her mother. She touched the necklace lightly, seeking courage in the memory of her mother to face the coming ordeal.

However, though Maude had hidden her scars, she knew they were there, the ugly marks which the *Ton* had decided made her unfit to mingle with society, a woman unfit for marriage and motherhood, an object to be scorned or pitied. The *Ton* that would shortly be descending upon her home in numbers.

Her hand trailed from the necklace to where the scars lay hidden beneath filmy lace, and the familiar anxiety threatened to overwhelm her. But she pushed it down determinedly, her fingers brushing the pearls once more.

Mother, I pray you, give me the strength this night to face my fears. For Ralph. For Damian, too. For myself.

Maude must have sensed her thoughts. "You look lovely, Milady," she said gently. "And your beautiful mask will disguise your face, so there's naught to fear."

"Hmm," Abby murmured, getting tired of being told not to be afraid. It seemed as if no one truly understood her feelings. *But how can they?*

A fancy box from Fortesque's Emporium was sitting on the bed, inside it a delicate mask fashioned in the likeness of a deer, a spotted doe. Abby had to hope it would be enough to protect her identity from prying eyes.

"You'll look very mysterious, Milady. No one will be thinking of anything but how lucky Mr. Ross is to be dancing with you, I'm sure," Maude said.

"I doubt that. He will have to ask me at least once, I suppose, to avoid being seen as rude. But I am not looking forward to it." That was a lie because she had been fantasizing about it for days. But she was nervous as well.

"Whyever not, Milady? You would be the envy of every young lady in the room," a surprised Maude exclaimed.

"I do not want their envy. And his appeal is exactly the problem. I admit I am not immune to his charms, and you know very well how difficult it is to keep my distance when I am near him. How much worse is it going to be when he is whirling me about the dance floor?"

"I see what you mean, Milady," Maude replied, sounding disappointed. "What a shame. I should love to dance with him."

"Then don my gown and mask and take my place," Abby suggested half seriously.

Maude giggled. "It's a lovely idea, but I fear they would be able to tell the difference between us. I do not have the air of gracious nobility as you do, Milady."

"You have more nobility in your little finger than some of the *Ton*, I assure you, Maude. They pretend to be civilized but many are savages underneath all the finery," Abby replied with feeling. "Besides all that, I am not sure I even remember the steps to all the dances. I have practiced a little with Claire, but we usually end up laughing too hard to continue."

That set Maude off giggling again.

"I just pray I do not make a fool of myself in front of Damian. If that happens, I shall simply die on the spot," Abby went on, perfectly serious despite Maude's laughter.

She was distracted by the sound of approaching carriage wheels. Her heart thudded in her chest.

"Oh, the guests are starting to arrive," she murmured, squeezing her hands tightly together. *I must not be afraid*, she told herself, trying not to feel bad for refusing to join Ralph in greeting the guests on arrival. As lady of the house, it was her duty, but it was a step too far, and she had put her foot down.

"Thank you, Maude," she whispered as the maid dabbed essence of rose behind her ears and on her wrists, then helped her into her satin dancing slippers. "You had better help me with the mask now. It is almost time for me to go down."

"Ooh, this is the part I have been looking forward to the most," the maid admitted, rushing to open the box and carefully lifting out the mask.

"It is surprisingly comfortable," Abby said, standing still while Maude fastened the black silk ribbons to affix the beautifully painted mask. Once it was done, she looked in the mirror, to see her own face transformed.

"It is magical, Milady. No one will ever guess it's you," Maude said, her cheeks pink with vicarious excitement.

Abby nodded, feeling a little reassured at the way the mask obscured her features almost completely. "It will do," she said. "And now, I suppose I had better go down."

At the top of the staircase, she paused and took a deep breath. The evening ahead loomed large in her mind—the music, the crowd, the expectations. As she slowly descended the stairs, she could hear the string quartet tuning up, the murmur of voices growing louder, the scent of roses and wax polish mingling in the air. The hall was alive with color and light.

It was terrifying.

She stopped hallway down, seeing a fleet of maids gathering the coats and outdoor paraphernalia of the incoming guests, all in their various disguises. The animal kingdom featured prominently among them, with others exotic, fanciful, and ornate, harking back to the romance of old Venice. Withers, in all his splendor, was directing the stream of people into the large reception room leading to the ballroom.

"Abby, there you are. I've been waiting for you. I thought you might like an escort."

At the sound of the familiar, deep voice, Abby looked down. A dashing masculine figure she knew well, dressed in tailored black evening clothes, a crisp white cravat at his throat, was standing near the base of the stairs looking up at her. From behind the velvet face of a black leopard, distinctive green eyes met hers.

For a heartbeat, the world stopped.

As she descended the rest of the way, behind the mask, she saw Damian's eyes widen in such frank appreciation, her breath caught in her throat.

When she reached him, he bowed slightly. "You look ..." He exhaled, apparently unable to finish.

Abby's blush of pleasure burned her cheeks. At the same time, she felt suddenly mischievous. "I am sorry, sir. I fear you have mistaken me for someone else. I do not think we have met," she said archly.

He laughed, a rich, hearty baritone that sent shivers through her, and his eyes twinkled through the mask.

With an extravagant bow, he said, "Mysterious, beautiful lady, forgive my poor manners in importuning you so rudely. I thought I recognized you, but I see I was wrong. However, now we are here, will you allow me the pleasure of escorting you to the ballroom and helping you to a glass of champagne? Or several?"

Behind her mask, she smiled. "I am not sure if I will be safe in your company. You appear to be a large jungle cat, a wild beast, in fact. Whereas I am a defenseless deer."

Where on earth is this coming from?! What am I doing? Oh, I cannot help it. I am flirting like a debutante. It is him, he has put a spell on me!

The green eyes flashed, setting her heart aflutter beneath her bodice. They stood quietly for a moment, oblivious to the milling people, the noise, the swell of music beginning in the background.

"My lady, I assure you, you have quite tamed this wild beast's heart. I could no more hurt you than boil my own head."

He said it so seriously, she had to stifle an unladylike snort of laughter, disguising it as a small cough.

"Since you ask so nicely, I shall give you the benefit of the doubt," she replied, stepping down next to him.

"Shall we?" he asked, gallantly offering her his arm. Abby stared at it, the implication of the outstretched limb giving her pause.

Propriety dictated that a single lady, if not engaged to a single gentleman, ought to avoid touching him. The fleeting touch of gloved hands while dancing or alighting from a carriage was permitted. But in the main, such intimacy was to be avoided, to protect a lady's reputation.

But we are in disguise. No one knows who we are. None can judge us.

She placed her hand gently on his sleeve. "Thank you, sir. I am quite thirsty."

As they crossed the threshold of the ballroom together, heads turned—and Abby found she did not mind the stares. Damian had said the mask would make her less fearful. He could hardly have known it, but it was having a much more powerful effect upon her than that.

Fearful of strangers she might be, reclusive she was. But she still had her rebellious streak, as her penchant for sporting scandalous divided skirts and riding astride proved. Now, in her guise as a gentle doe, she found some of her old courage, determined to do her duty and face the *Ton* with her head held high.

Admittedly, walking in on the arm of such an impressive gentleman helped as well.

* * *

The ballroom at Worsley House sparkled like a jewel under the soft glow of a hundred flickering candles. Crystal chandeliers hung from the vaulted ceiling, their prisms scattering light like miniature rainbows across the polished parquet floor.

The walls, draped in swathes of bright oriental silks woven with garlands of greenery, entwined with exotic, brightly colored hothouse flowers was a feast for the eyes, echoing the richly adorned gowns of the ladies. The scent of fresh roses and orange blossom mingled with gardenia, sandalwood, and lemon, creating an inviting, intoxicating atmosphere that both calmed and excited Damian.

"The décor is splendid, Abby. You have an artist's eye, I think," he told the gorgeous little woman on his arm, proud to be the one to escort her. Offering her his arm had been a risk, against all propriety. But he knew Abby was much more than her fears and took a chance.

When she had placed her gloved hand on his arm, a powerful tremor had gone through him that was far more than mere gratification at knowing he had judged her correctly. *Yes, the mask is doing the trick, all right.*

"Thank you," she replied, giving a low chuckle that warmed his heart, "but I cannot claim all the credit. My good friend Miss Potter came up with the idea and was a great help to me. I am not very accomplished, I am afraid, and about as artistic as a horse," she admitted.

"You must meet her. She is here somewhere. Look out for a snowy owl."

"It will be an honor to meet any friend of yours," he replied, meaning every word. "I hope to introduce you to one of mine." He meant Lyle, curious as to what he would make of Abby.

Her eyes glowed gratifyingly. "That will be ... interesting, I'm sure."

"There is one thing I would ask before the music begins," he said, meeting her eyes, hearing her slight sharp intake of breath.

She knows what I am about to say. Is she as excited about it as I am?

"Oh? And what is that?"

"Dance the first set with me."

There was a silence while her gaze searched his. He felt a flash of fear. *Is she going to refuse me?*

But suddenly, her eyes smiled, and his fear melted into elation. She held out her wrist, her dance card dangling from its cord. "Very well. You had better fill in your name then."

Using the tiny pencil provided, he scrawled his initial with a flourish, feeling a sense of accomplishment. His plans for the first part of the evening were going smoothly so far. However, how it progressed after that was not entirely in his hands. Much as he hated the idea of Abby dancing with other partners, he knew it was expected, and that he could do nothing to change it.

He not only intended to dance the first set with her, hoping to make a good impression, but a second as well. And if, when he asked her, she accepted, then it would mean she acknowledged that his interest in her was genuine ... and welcomed it. Then, he would ask her a third time. If she accepted again, then the whole room, including her brother, would expect an engagement to be announced shortly. The idea made him tingle all over.

"Oh, look, there is Ralph. Oh dear, he's not exactly incognito, is he?" Abby suddenly observed with a chuckle.

Damian followed her eyeline and spotted Ralph. His friend was in evening dress, settled in his bathchair, a half-drunk glass of champagne in one hand. He had pushed his wolf mask up onto his head and was engaged in animated conversation with a group of people.

Damian knew the signs and noticed with interest that Ralph was paying particular attention to a statuesque blond in pale-blue satin, wearing the mask of a brilliant bird. The pair were engaged in animated conversation. Damian supposed the older couple with them were her parents.

Well, well, well, I've never seen that look in his eyes before. This could be serious. I wonder who she is.

He snagged a couple of glasses of champagne from a passing tray and presented one to Abby. She sipped at it, he fancied, as a bee sips nectar from a flower. *Lord, I really am turning into a romantic,* he thought, curious to discover he did not mind at all. *It is her. This is what she does to me. She is slowly turning me into a poet.*

Indeed, his arm was tingling where hers was resting on it, her touch light as thistledown yet hot as fire.

"Who is that young lady he is talking to? Do you know her?" Abby asked, also watching her brother, her bright, gray eyes filled with curiosity behind her charming doe-like features.

"No, I have never seen her before, but I think Ralph is rather taken with her," he replied, pleased for his friend. He had known Ralph for years and knew he had a soft heart. In fact, he had often teased him about it. *And now here am, I am waxing lyrical over his sister. What a strange world it is!*

"She looks very nice. I am curious to meet her," she murmured, an edge of uncertainty in her voice that made him wonder what she was thinking.

"Shall we go and quiz him about it?" Damian asked.

But there was no time for Abby to reply. At that moment, the Master of Ceremonies for the evening, their neighbor, Sir Timothy Gallant, the famous marine engineer, got up in front of the musicians and tinged a spoon against his glass. He had been co-opted to do the honors since Ralph was *hors de combat,* so to speak, and Damian was incognito.

The ringing chimes drew the attention of the guests.

"I am pleased to announce, ladies and gentlemen, that the dance floor will shortly open. Please find your partners for the first set. As the program states, it comprises three different waltzes," Sir Timothy announced, to the guests' general appreciation.

Damian smiled secretly at that. Being in charge of organizing the music and determined to be the first to dance with Abby, he had planned it that way. A dance set could last up to twenty minutes, twenty glorious minutes of being as close to Abby as he could possibly get without actually embracing her.

Several other gentlemen approached her, asking to fill in her dance card. Damian eyed them suspiciously, wondering who was hiding behind the masks. Men he probably knew, had even invited. It did not help that she removed her hand from his arm to respond to the would-be dance partners.

Suddenly, for the first time in his life, he was gripped by a powerful emotion he realized must be jealousy.

Its intensity shook him as he was forced to stand and watch, gritting his teeth behind his mask, while the others complimented her extravagantly and scribbled down their names for forthcoming dances.

Unfortunately, though he tried, he could not make any of the scribbles out. Not that he knew what he would do if he had. These people were potential buyers, investors. Upsetting them was out of the question.

Nevertheless, he was shocked by how hard he had to fight down the urge to snatch the card from her wrist and rip it in two.

Watching the exchanges closely, he noticed a tremor in Abby's hand as she held out the card to be signed. It was small, but he was so finely tuned to her every move, he saw it. Concern for her cooled his jealousy somewhat. She was nervous, uncomfortable, embarrassed by the compliments. However, her innate good manners and sense of duty overcame her anxiety, and she was perfectly polite to all comers.

It was a little solace to him to know that he alone knew how she was truly feeling. His admiration for the way she was managing her fears only grew. Yet a little prickle of jealousy remained.

"You have attracted a lot of attention ... from other gentlemen," he heard himself say.

"I did not expect it. It was quite a shock. I have not been among the *Ton* like this for ... a very long time," she replied innocently, a small tremor in her voice. Doubt showed in her eyes. "I confess, it has been so long, I fear those gentlemen will be very disappointed with my dancing. I have likely forgotten all the steps and shall tread on their toes and make a fool of myself." She laughed uneasily.

"I shan't mind having my toes trodden on," he told her, his jealousy dying away, wanting to soothe her worries. "And I have every confidence the steps will come back to you once we take to the floor. Dancing is a little like riding a horse, I always think. Once learned, you never forget."

"I wish I could share your confidence."

The opening strains of the first set filled the room, and the dance floor began to fill. He led her out. Damian held his breath as they got into position. He laid his left hand reverently on the curve of her waist, thrilled to feel the warm softness beneath. Their right hands clasped, the fingers entwining as the dance demanded. Abby looked up at him with wide, trusting eyes, having no idea of how stunning she was or the effect she was having on him.

It feels so right!

The music swelled, and he swept her away, glorying in the feel of her in his arms, twirling her about, marveling at how light on her feet she was. And she never made the slightest misstep. She was grace in motion, and he noticed over her head how many looks they were attracting. Looks of approval and curiosity.

"You dance beautifully, Abby. You see, I was right. You have not forgotten a single step," he said softly, careful not to disturb the rhythm. "I could do this all night."

He knew that beneath her mask, she was blushing by the way the tips of her ears turned pink. "Thank you, but I fear you are too kind. I am lucky to have such a forgiving partner," she said, typically deprecating.

His heart fluttered. She was so unlike the other ladies here—no artifice, no falseness. Just humble honesty and a courage that shone quietly.

Damian tightened his hold just a fraction, guiding her through the steps with a tenderness he hadn't known he possessed. "Abby, I don't want to be just a good partner," he said, voice low. "I want to be the only partner."

She tensed in his arms, and he wondered if he had gone too far and frightened her. Her silvery eyes searched his, wide and vulnerable, as if weighing the truth of his words.

"Do not say that," she whispered, barely audible.

"Why not? It is the truth."

"Just, please, Damian, do not toy with me."

"I am sad you would even entertain the idea," he replied without heat, not expecting it would be easy to convince her of his seriousness.

The orchestra shifted to a slower melody, a French waltz that invited closeness and quiet moments. Damian pulled her gently closer, every nerve alive to the warmth of her body, the faint scent of roses in her hair. For a while, the noisy world faded, leaving only the two of them swaying under the watchful eyes of chandeliers and curious glances.

Across the room, he recognized Lyle, his features obscured by a mask resembling a bear. His friend towered over the knot of people he was with, his mop of sandy hair distinctive. Their eyes met. Lyle, obviously recognizing him too, gave him a slow nod and raised his glass in silent salute.

Damian nodded back, excited to see him.

Naturally, Lyle had been one of the first on the guest list. He had sent back his acceptance along with a brief note for Damian, saying he had "interesting news to impart on that subject we discussed," and promising to do so in person at the ball. Damian prayed he was at last going to find out the riddle of Abby's reclusivity, which he believed was the key to winning her heart.

But it will have to wait until after this set.

When, to his great regret, the set finally came to an end, loath to let Abby go, he led her from the floor.

"Would you like some punch?" he asked, meaning to keep her as long as he could.

"Yes, please, that would be very refreshing," she said. He left her scanning the crowd for her friend Miss Potter and went to the refreshment tables. Lyle was still nearby, and he hoped to speak to him quickly whilst fetching the drinks.

They greeted each other warmly and moved to one side so they could talk alone.

"Is that her?"

"Yes."

"I can see why you're so smitten, but are you truly serious about her?"

"I've never been so serious about anything in my life."

"I thought so," Lyle said, his disappointment obvious. "I want you to know you're letting the side down badly. What about all those promises you made, about never getting entangled? What about freedom? A misspent bachelorhood? What about me, your loyal friend?"

"Blast bachelorhood, and I care naught for those hurt feelings you pretend to feel. I know you have no feelings in you," Damian replied, hardly knowing what he was saying as he poured two glasses of punch. His eyes barely left Abby. He did not want any other gentlemen butting in. But he had to know. "Now, hurry up and tell me what I need to know. I don't have much time. I'm in love. For the first time. I don't want anyone else to snatch her away."

It felt heady to speak the words aloud for the first time. Warmth spread through his chest. It was true. He was hopelessly, utterly enchanted.

Lyle groaned. "I knew it! This is a disaster."

Damian took no notice. He was watching Abby through the crowd and saw a woman, the same woman he had noticed earlier, come up to her. She appeared to whisper something to Abby.

"Well, it took a bit of digging without giving the game away. It was Mother who—"

But Damian was not listening. Instead, he was transfixed by Abby's reaction to whatever it was the woman has said. The woman moved away and was lost in the crowd. Abby, face chalk white, posture stiff, headed for the garden doors and disappeared through them.

"I have to go," he muttered, filled with a sense of urgency to follow her. He put down the glasses of punch, oblivious to Lyle's surprise. Worry tightened around him like a vice as he hurried after Abby.

She was not among the people taking in the mild night air on the terrace, so he knew she must have gone into the garden. Determined to find her, he went down the steps.

His shoes made soft thuds against the polished stone path. The garden at night was a different world—cool and mysterious. The moon cast a silvery glow over beds of blooming lilies and roses, their petals heavy with dew. The scent of jasmine curled around him, and the rustle of leaves whispered secrets in the gentle breeze.

But none of it meant anything to him. Finding Abby was his only objective.

Finally, under the sprawling branches of an ancient oak, he found her sitting alone on a wooden bench. He was dismayed to see her shoulders were shaking with silent sobs. Moonlight glinted on the tears streaking her cheeks.

"Abby," he said softly, stepping closer.

She startled at his voice but did not move away, only dabbed at her tears with a handkerchief.

Her mask lay next to her on the seat. "We should not be out here alone," she whispered, her voice fragile. "If anyone sees—"

"Let them," Damian interrupted, sitting beside her, pulling off his mask and taking her hands in his. "I'm not worried about gossip or scandal. Let them say what they want."

She removed her hands from his. "What about my reputation? Do you care about that?"

"Of course."

"Then you should go, or they will force you to marry me."

"Oh, how awful," he said drily, unable to help himself.

She looked at him sharply, her eyes swimming with unshed tears. "You are jesting. But you do not know what you are saying."

"I assure you, I have not drunk so much champagne that I do not have all my wits about me. I refuse to leave you in this state. It pains me to see you like this. What has upset you? Who has upset you? Tell me and I shall go and maul them with my claws and rend them with my fangs."

He was pleased to see the corners of her lips twitch. But then they turned down again, and his heart fell.

Her sharp look turned to uncertainty. "I— I cannot say. It was nothing. A chance remark, that is all."

"Clearly, it was more than that. I saw that woman who whispered to you. Something unkind, I deduce. Whatever it was, I am sure it was born out of jealousy. Take no notice."

She shook her head. A tear fell from the tip of her nose, and his heart swelled towards her.

"Abby, tell me, I beg you. I cannot bear to see you like this. Surely, you know you can trust me by now? I would protect you, not hurt you," he insisted.

"You don't understand, Damian. I— I'm not like the other ladies in there. You would not be so kind if you knew the truth about me."

He shook his head fiercely. "No. You're wrong. Trust me. I am very good at keeping secrets. I give you my word I will never hurt you if I can help it."

She hesitated, the vulnerability in her eyes rousing his protective instincts to fever pitch.

Then, she seemed to decide something. "Very well. Since you are so insistent ... we shall see what your word means."

He held his breath as, with trembling fingers, she slowly pushed back her hair from her shoulder, exposing her neck, and lowered the neckline of her dress as far as was decent.

He stared at the puckered patch of scarring that ran in a narrow strip from beneath one ear, then widened as it spread down her shoulder and the top of her arm, almost to the elbow. It stood out starkly against the smooth, whiteness of the surrounding skin.

So, this is her secret, Damian thought, letting out a long breath as he continued to look at the scars, which were obviously from being burned. The fire, the pain, the suffering she had endured—it was all etched into her skin.

Overwhelmed that she trusted him enough to show him her truth, before he knew what he was doing, he leaned forward and pressed a gentle kiss to the scarred flesh of her shoulder.

Chapter Twenty

Abby's eyes widened in surprise, then softened with tears. "You're not repulsed? Sorry for me?" she asked, her voice cracking.

He shook his head, voice low and certain. "I'm neither of those things," he breathed, "Your scars, they just make you more beautiful to me."

Swept by powerful emotions she could hardly name, she felt her lips tremble as she looked up at him, searching his face uncertainly, wanting so much to believe what she saw reflected there. He seemed so in earnest, yet her doubts persisted.

"I admire you even more now you have shared your secret with me, Abby," he said, voice thick with emotion. "Thank you for trusting me to keep it. Do you feel like telling me how you came by your scars?"

"It is a long story."

"I have all the time in the world."

"Very well, I shall tell you."

He listened intently as she laid out her tragic history, by turns sorrowful and outraged by what had happened to her, how bravely she had borne it all, and how badly the *Ton* had treated her.

When she had finished, Damian was profoundly moved. He looked intently into her eyes. "Abby, you risked your life to save those horses. You fought through pain and fear and came through stronger. Those scars—they're a badge of your love and bravery."

She swallowed hard, a fragile smile beginning to bloom on her lips, like a flower breaking through stone.

"I never thought anyone would see me like that," she whispered, wanting so much to believe him.

Then, Damian cupped her face with his hands, his thumbs brushing away her tears. She let him, closing her eyes briefly, reveling in the warmth radiating from his touch.

She opened them when he whispered, "I see you, Abby. The real you. And I want to be the one to protect you, always."

A lump rose in her throat. "Do you really mean it, Damian?" she asked with difficulty, caught up in his beautiful green eyes that shone with sincerity.

"Never doubt that I mean it. Whatever happens," he whispered, "I'm here. For you."

A wave of joy, of relief washed over her, and she leaned against him, resting her head on his chest while he held her tenderly. "Thank you, Damian. Thank you for saying those things."

They remained like that, the night wrapped around them, a cocoon of moonlight and quiet, contented breaths. She could hear his heart beating in his chest and allowed her hopes to soar, allowed herself to experience for the first time the true happiness she had never imagined could be hers.

And the cause of her happiness was Damian Ross.

"Well, if you feel up to it, we had better do our duty and go back inside," he said eventually. "The ball is still in full swing, and we have yet to have our second dance."

"You would dance with me twice?" she asked, thrills chasing up and down her spine.

"I was banking on it," he said, smiling down at her and stroking her hair.

Realizing he was serious, she laughed, amazed at the way the situation has turned around. She suddenly felt like the bravest, most beautiful woman in the world, thanks to the wonderful, handsome man with the kind green eyes in front of her. "In that case, it would be rude of me to refuse."

The garden shimmered in the moonlight as Abby walked beside Damian beneath a canopy of trailing wisteria and silvery branches, her hand on his sleeve. The music from the ballroom drifted through the open garden doors, a soft echo of violins and laughter that barely touched the stillness of the evening.

She had dreamed of nights like this once, long ago—before the fire, before shame had made her retreat into herself. But now, walking in the quiet with Damian's hand warm against hers, it didn't feel like a dream. It felt real. Solid. Astonishing.

He stopped beneath a flowering arch and turned to face her. His gaze caught hers with a gravity that sent a ripple through her chest.

"Abby," he said, his voice low and thick with something unspoken. "I hope you know what it meant to me, that you shared that part of yourself."

The moonlight caught in his eyes. Sincere. Reverent. She looked away for a heartbeat, overwhelmed.

"You're one of the very few who know," she said softly. "I don't speak of it. Not because I'm ashamed any longer, but because it's exhausting to explain."

He reached for her hand again, brushing his thumb against the inside of her wrist. "You don't need to explain. Not to me."

His touch was light, almost reverent. Intoxicating. He leaned closer, so close she could feel his breath against her cheek. "I meant what I said back there. About your strength. And about you being beautiful."

On impulse, she stood on tiptoes and pressed her lips to his. She thought she would always remember his look of delight at that moment. The kiss felt like a return, not a beginning—like something she had lost a long time ago, which Damian had finally helped her reclaim.

"Who was that woman who upset you, Abby?" he asked.

"Did you not recognize her? You have met her before, at the horse fair," she replied. "She is Lady Araminta Greene."

It came back to him. "Of course! I thought there was something familiar about her. What did she say?"

"She said I had no right to be flaunting myself in public, that everyone knew of my disfigurement and was talking about it."

Anger flowed through Damian. "What a spiteful little madam," he said through gritted teeth. "She's clearly jealous of your beauty, Abby. That's why she wanted to hurt you. It was she who upset you at the horse fair, wasn't it?"

Abby nodded in conformation, and he went on angrily, "I thought so. She should think herself lucky she's not a man. I would challenge her to a duel if she were."

Abby was deeply touched by his reaction and squeezed his fingers with hers. "I would not want you to risk your life like that on my account. I admit, I let her words hurt me. But now, I care nothing for them. I am sorry for her that she is so miserable as to wish to harm others."

"That's my Abby," he said approvingly, squeezing her hand back.

They were approaching the terrace steps. Damian halted them in the shadows nearby, outside the circle of light emanating from above. Music, chatter, and laughter drifted on the breeze.

"You go in first, and I'll follow in a few minutes," he told her as they helped each other with their masks. "But remember, the next set is mine."

"All right," she agreed, adjusting her mask. "We shall meet by the dance floor."

When they parted, her pulse was fluttering like the wings of a caged bird, but it was no longer driven by fear. It was possibility. A sense of self she thought had burned away forever.

When they met once more in the ballroom a short while later, Abby felt as though she were looking at the room with new eyes. It seemed brighter than before, the music more beautiful, the people more welcoming.

They drank some punch, and when the next set came around, they took to the floor again. Heads turned. Eyes followed. Abby did not care. She was elated, and she threw herself into the sheer pleasure of being in Damian's arms.

Ralph was parked, waiting to meet them when they finally stepped off the floor, his smile wide. Abby was surprised to see the blonde lady in blue silk standing with him. She was still wearing her mask, but there was something in her pose—one hand resting on the arm of the bathchair—that hinted at possession.

"You two looked magnificent out there," Ralph said in greeting. "I wanted to catch you before you go dashing off having fun. I want to introduce you both to someone," he went on, his eyes sparkling as he smiled up at his companion.

"Abby, this is Lady Caroline Booth. Caroline, this is my sister, Abigail. But keep that under your hat. She's incognito tonight. And this savage-looking beast is my friend and partner, Damian Ross."

Lady Caroline curtsied with elegance but none of the aloofness Abby had come to expect from society's darlings. She pushed up her mask slightly. Her smile was warm, her pale blue eyes bright with good humor.

"It's such a pleasure to meet you, Lady Abby," she said. "Ralph has told me you are the soul of Worsley Hall. I've been dying to see the gardens."

"Then you must come in the morning; it is at its best then," Abby replied, unexpectedly charmed. "Everything is just coming into bloom. I am sure Ralph would love to give you a tour."

She watched Ralph glance at Lady Caroline when he thought no one noticed, a look of pure affection. It was very like the look Damian had recently given her in the garden. She had always been scared of what would happen to her when Ralph married and she had to hand the household keys over to his wife. But fortified with Damian's devotion, she only felt happy for her brother.

They talked a while longer before Ralph wanted some punch, whereupon an obliging Caroline wheeled him away to the refreshments table

Abby turned to Damian, her heart impossibly full.

"You know," she said, her voice low, "I think this is the happiest I've been since before the fire. Since ever."

He looked at her then, not just with affection, but with something deeper. Reverence. Hope. Her heart felt like it would explode with happiness.

"Then I'm glad," he said. "Because you deserve every bit of it."

She looked up at him, her chest full of something too big for words. "I have you to thank for that," she said simply.

In his answering smile, she saw the promise of the lasting happiness she had previously only dreamed of, and her hopes soared like a bird.

When she found Claire and her father and introduced them to Damian, he was the perfect gentleman, complimenting Claire on her good taste with the decor. Abby could not help but be proud of him. She smiled to see Claire's eyes growing round with delight as he praised her good taste.

While the two men were speaking, Claire whispered to her, "I see now why you were so confused. I have yet to see his face, but he is an imposing specimen indeed."

"His face will not disappoint, I assure you," Abby whispered back, quickly giving her friend an excited run-down of what had happened in the garden.

"My, that is the most romantic thing I have ever heard," Claire declared, her hand to her chest, secretly eyeing Damian with wonder. "I am ecstatic for you, my dear Abby. I truly wish the path of love runs smoothly for both of you. You know I wish you every happiness."

"Thank you. I admit, I am very excited about how things may progress. I feel as if I am dreaming. If I am, then I hope I never wake up."

"You are not dreaming. It is all true," Claire whispered back, giving her arm a gentle squeeze. "Just let yourself believe."

The next set came around, and the girls had to part to fulfill their obligations to their dance partners. And when Damian met Abby coming off the floor, commandeering her as soon as her partner left her, he said, "I have a friend I want you to meet, too."

"I am excited and honored to meet anyone who is your friend, Damian. If you value them, then I know they must be good," she said, letting him steer her towards a very tall, well-built man with a shock of sandy hair sprouting above his bear's head mask. He held a glass of champagne and was standing quietly on the edge of a small group of chattering people.

The great bear of a man saw them approaching and turned to them, stepping away from the group.

"We meet at last, my friend," he greeted Damian cheerfully, lifting his mask.

"It's good to see you, my friend. Thank you for coming."

"I saw you on the dance floor, old fellow. Three waltzes, eh? Magnifique!" He slapped Damian on the shoulder. Then he looked directly at Abby and smiled.

"Abby, it's my somewhat dubious pleasure to introduce you to Lyle Bruton, one of my closest friends. Lyle, this is Lady Abigail Lucas, Ralph's sister."

The giant bowed elegantly. "Lady Abigail, I am charmed to make your acquaintance. Ralph is a treasured friend of mine. I feel as though I know you. I have heard so much about you from Damian here," he said in a rich, cultured voice.

"Oh?" Abby flicked a glance at Damian, flattered to think he had been talking about her with his friend. His eyes were smiling.

Reassured, she answered jokingly, "All good things, I hope."

"The utmost praise, I assure you," Lyle said. "And if you will forgive me for being forward, it is easy to see why. May I say how stunning you look?"

Abby saw a pair of twinkling hazel eyes peeking out from behind the mask. They seemed to brim with bonhomie, and she instantly warmed to the giant of a man beneath.

"Thank you, that is kind. Regrettably, he has told me nothing of you."

"I am not surprised. That is typically selfish of him," Lyle said drily. "But now we have met, I am sure we shall become firm friends."

"I do not doubt it," she said, eager to get to know Lyle better, feeling that if she did, she would feel even closer to Damian.

The rest of the evening passed in a whirl of dutiful dancing with her scheduled partners. In truth, she had eyes for no one but Damian and was absurdly pleased when he danced with no one else all evening.

His eyes never left her, and between sets, they would gravitate back together and resume their conversation, no longer hampered by the secrets of her past.

There is nothing more to fear, she thought, her soul as light as air.

When she eventually retired to bed in the early hours, they said a quiet, tender good night, and she slipped away to her chambers.

That night, in bed, instead of the familiar nightmares, her dreams were full of music and laughter, of being in Damian's arms, of hearing the wonderful words of affection he had spoken so earnestly. Words that had lit up her lonely world with joy.

Chapter Twenty-One

Damian could not sleep. His whole being thrummed with energy as he stood in the stable yard, his fine coat slung over his shoulder, and watched the first light of dawn spilling over the hills, brushing the mist-laced pastures with silver and gold.

The world around him was hushed, suspended in a moment between night and day. Inside the quiet sanctuary of the stables, he was alone. He moved with deliberate ease, soothed by the sounds of the horses and the rhythmic tsk-tsk of the curry comb as he ran it over Alba's white flanks.

The scent of hay, warm horseflesh, and saddle soap hung in the air—a grounding aroma that always helped him think. The familiar task soothed the storm within him, but this morning was like no other he had ever experienced.

His world felt totally changed. He felt changed, truly alive, his thoughts and emotions churning inside him.

I love her.

There was no longer any room for doubt, no shadow of hesitation. Abby—her courage, her intelligence, the graceful way she carried her scars—had claimed his heart so completely that he could barely remember a time when she wasn't at the center of his thoughts. Every glance she gave him, every word, every smile—each left an imprint deeper than the last.

He paused, resting his hand on the mare's neck. She nudged him affectionately with her nose, but he didn't smile as he usually would.

You can't keep lying to her.

The truth pressed against his chest like a stone. He leaned against the stall door, staring out toward the trees beyond the paddock. The early birds were just beginning their songs, tentative and sweet, as though unsure if the day had truly begun.

She deserves to know who you are. About Father. All of it.

He knew he had to tell her that he was not just plain Mr. Damian Ross, that he was Damian Ross, the Viscount Amberly, first son and heir to the Earl of Chartringham, one of the richest and most powerful political figures in the land. And he was not sure how she would react when he confessed that he had been lying to her all along.

He picked up a worn halter from its hook and ran his fingers along the leather, feeling each scuff and crease. The horses didn't care who he was. And Abby ... she had looked at him with trust.

Such trust, he knew, had to be met with the unvarnished truth. He prayed she would understand and forgive him.

He thought back to the final argument with his father. The study had smelled of pipe smoke and brandy. His father's voice had been clipped, full of cold fury.

"You would throw away everything—your name, your inheritance, your duty—for what? Some foolish ideal of independence?"

"I'd rather be a free man than a titled coward," Damian had replied, his voice shaking.

"Show some respect, boy!"

"I'm afraid it's too late for that, Father. I lost my respect for you the moment you married that woman," Damian shot back, referring to Mariah, his stepmother. She was barely older than he. "I've tried to ignore it, for your sake. But I can do so no longer. Nor can I stay under this roof while she is here. She's using you, but you're too blinded by her wiles to see it."

"How dare you speak of her in that manner?" the Earl growled.

"I do not wish to speak of her at all. I am leaving. For good."

"Leave if you must, boy. But remember, Chartringham, the title, everything, it will all be yours one day. You cannot walk away from your birthright," the old man had sputtered furiously.

"Watch me."

That had been eighteen months ago. He had left that night and never returned. At first, he had thought he might find peace in distance, in work, in simplicity. And for a while, he had. But the deep wound left by the estrangement remained raw. His heart had essentially been dead, and he had expected nothing more.

Until coming to Worsley ... and Abby.

She deserves a man who's honest, not one hiding behind a false persona. She needs to know who she's marrying.

But even as the conviction settled in his chest, fear snaked in its wake.

What if she doesn't forgive me? What if I tell her the truth ... and lose her forever?

He resolved to get her alone somewhere private that day, as soon as possible. If she forgave him and all was well, he intended to speak to Ralph as soon as possible and gain his permission to ask for her hand.

He strode towards the house, intending to rest for a couple of hours before making himself presentable for the momentous day ahead, a prayer of love and hope lodged firmly in his chest.

* * *

Abby floated along the landing towards the staircase, ready to greet the overnight guests cheerfully at breakfast, minus her mask this time.

She felt reborn, confident, happy, secure in Damian's love. She could not wait to see him.

At the top of the staircase, she heard voices below in the hall. She stopped, recognizing her brother's voice speaking quietly. She peered through the bannisters and looked down.

Ralph was in his bathchair, talking to a man dressed in dark clothing holding a satchel, whom she had never seen before.

Not wishing to interrupt, she waited patiently for them to finish, assuming the man was on his way out. As she waited, their voices floated up to her, and she could not avoid eavesdropping on their conversation. And the more she heard, the closer she listened. And the colder her blood ran.

As the two men finished their business, Abby turned numbly and rushed back to her chambers, shutting the door behind her. She leaned against it, agonized sobs tearing from her throat, seeing her dreams of happiness crumbling all around her.

* * *

Later that morning, the heavy oak door of Ralph's study creaked open, the familiar scent of leather-bound books and pipe tobacco wrapping around Damian like a worn cloak. Ralph was sitting in his bath chair behind his desk, the small silver bell he used to summon assistance resting on some papers.

"Damian," he said, looking up, his expression unusually serious.

"Ralph," Damian responded, arranging himself in an arm chair. "Is all well? You look rather concerned about something."

"I am not concerned for myself, but for you, my dear chap. A man was here earlier. A lawyer, name of Garland."

The name struck a note of dread in Damian's heart. Garland handled all his family's legal business. "Garland works for Father." He clenched his fists. "I'd like to know how he tracked me down."

"I have no clue, but I claimed ignorance of your presence, told him he was misinformed and sent him away."

Relief flowed through Damian, but beneath it, anger and dread still lingered. "Thanks, I'm grateful. Do you think Garland believed you?"

Ralph shook his head. "Sadly no. After he left, I found this letter on my desk. It's addressed to you." He handed over a sealed envelope.

"It's the old man's seal all right. Oh, God! What does he want?" Damian growled, his stomach trying in knots. Full of trepidation, he opened the letter and started to read.

"My son, if you receive this, know that time grows short. I am gravely ill and burdened with regret for our estrangement. I beg you to return to Worsley, to reconcile before it is too late."

The letter felt heavy in Damian's hands. A thousand emotions collided within him: anger, sorrow, guilt, confusion.

He looked at Ralph. "He's very sick, he says. He wants me to come home. After all this time."

"Yes, Garland told me that much, and I was sorry to hear it," Ralph said softly. "What will you do?"

Damian clenched his jaw, in an agony of indecision. "I don't know yet. This is all such a shock." He got up and began pacing the room, the letter clenched in his fist. "I need to think. I can't just ride back there and pretend nothing's happened. This could not have come at a worse time."

Ralph nodded sympathetically. "Take what time you need to decide. But my advice is don't delay too long. Regret is a bitter companion."

Damian sighed heavily, the weight of the news settling over him.

Buy whether I agree to go or not, I cannot leave Worsley without first telling Abby the truth about everything.

* * *

Knowing Abby would be coming to the stables at some point, he decided to wait there, to tell her everything face to face.

The familiar smells of hay, leather, and horse mingled with the faint musk of early summer blooms came drifting through the open doors. The quiet murmur of stable hands at work formed a soft backdrop to his thoughts as he tried to distract himself by checking on Flame and Spirit.

But all the time, he was waiting for Abby, willing her to come and put an end to his uncertainty. One way or the other.

He heard light footsteps approaching. Recognizing them instantly, his heart leapt into his mouth. *She's coming!*

Not wishing for them to be overhead, he went out to meet her. She stopped when she saw him. He was just about to call out to her when he saw her face, white and pinched, her lips a thin line. Her eyes were red, as if she had been crying. He wondered if Araminta had anything to do with it. But then his heart lurched with fear. *Or has she changed her mind about me overnight?*

He hurried over to her. "Abby, are you all right? Has something happened?" he asked, peering at her in concern.

"Yes, you happened. Lord Damain Ross, Viscount Amberley, son and heir to Lord Ross, the Earl of Chartringham," she said, her voice full of bitter accusation.

The shock of realization hit him like a blow to the chest. *She knows!*

"Abby, I can explain everything," he tried to say, but she began walking away from him, back towards the house, chin proudly in the air.

"Explain until you are blue in the face. I refuse to listen to anything you have to say. You are a liar. You have done nothing but lie to me the whole time you have been here," she said, the ice maiden once more.

He followed her, his stomach churning with fear. "Please, Abby, listen to me. I didn't mean to lie to you. Let me just tell you why I had to do it."

She kept walking towards the house. "No. I will not listen to another word from you. You duped me. Played me like a fool. And I *have* been a fool. Go away." Her voice cracked, and he could hear tears in it.

But he was close to tears himself. "Abby, please, just hear me out," he begged, panicking as she reached the rear door of the house, refusing to even look at him.

"How could you?" she burst out as she wrenched the door open, looking at him for the first time. Full of pain and fury, her eyes flashed like daggers, stabbing at him.

His heart stuttered. "Abby—"

"No!" she cut him off. "I overheard the lawyer. That is how I learned who you really are and that you've been deceiving me all along!"

"But it wasn't like that, Abby, I promise. I never meant to hurt you. I was waiting for you in the stables just now. After last night, I knew I had to tell you everything," he pleaded.

"Last night! You must have found it very amusing, watching me be taken in by your sweet lies. I am such an idiot. I trusted you so much, I even showed you . . ." She stopped, tears rolling down her cheeks. "Oh, what does it matter now? It is all ruined anyway."

"Abby, just give me a minute to explain," he begged again, pain flaring in his chest, reaching for her arm. But she evaded his grasp.

"Go away. I never want to see you again as long as I live!"

With that she stepped inside and slammed the door, leaving him standing there, numb with shock.

Chapter Twenty-Two

The moment she slammed the door to her chambers shut behind her, Abby's resolve shattered like brittle glass. She leaned against the heavy oak, her breath coming in shallow, ragged gasps. The truth—Damian's truth—pressed down on her chest like a relentless storm.

What an idiot I have been, taken in by a handsome face and a charming smile. What right did I, cursed and blighted as I am, have to think that happiness could be mine?

Her fingers trembled as she brushed the tears away, trying to hold herself together. But the sadness was too heavy. Too raw.

Maude came in through the door, carrying a pile of clean linen. Immediately noticing Abby's distress, she hastily put the linen on the bed and rushed over to where she was sitting at the vanity.

"Milady, what is it?" she asked gently, hesitating before gently touching her mistress's trembling arms. "When I left you earlier, you were walking on air. What has happened to upset you so in so short a time?"

Abby's voice broke. "I ... I overheard something this morning, Maude. Something terrible."

Maude's brow furrowed with concern. "What is it, Milady? You can tell me. Maybe I can help."

Abby's shoulders drooped. "Damian. He is not who I was led to believe he is. He is not just a humble gentleman. He's the Viscount of Amberley, the Earl of Chartringham's son—the heir."

Maude blinked, absorbing the news. "My stars. Well, I'm not surprised to learn he's a nobleman. He's a gentleman of the first water. But why is it so terrible? Surely, it doesn't mean he loves you any less, does it?"

Abby shook her head fiercely. "That's just it, Maude. I don't know what to believe anymore. How long has he been lying? How many parts of his life has he hidden? I showed him everything—my scars, my fears. I trusted him with the pieces of myself I've hidden from the world. But it was all a game to him. He played me like the fool I am," she sobbed.

Maude crouched beside her. "You mustn't think that, Milady. You are not a fool. Mr. Ross, I mean, Lord Ross, doesn't strike me as the kind of gentleman who would toy with your feelings. He's not the sort to treat true love as a game. If he lied to you, he may have had good reason. Has he explained himself to you?"

"He tried to, but I refused to listen to him. How can I trust him now? If he can keep something so important from me, what else is he hiding? He's a nobleman, with all the power and choice that brings. He has all the ladies of the *Ton* to choose from. You said yourself he likely has hordes of them chasing after him. Why would he pick on me but for his own amusement?"

A fresh wave of tears spilled down her cheeks. "I thought— God, I thought maybe after the fire, after all I've lost, I had a chance of finally finding lasting happiness. But I was right to be afraid. I knew it was dangerous to let my guard down and trust him. And now what I feared the most has happened. The happiness I stupidly believed could be mine has been snatched away again, like a cruel joke."

"You're not alone, Milady. You have friends who care. The master for one," Maude tried to comfort her.

Abby gave a hollow laugh. "Oh, yes, my dear brother. I thought he was on my side. But he knew Damian's real identity all along. He didn't tell me either."

"Perhaps he thought he was protecting you, Milady. Or perhaps Mr. Ross swore him to secrecy. Without knowing the true circumstances, we cannot know. But I'm sure the master believed he was doing the right thing and never intended you to get hurt."

"But it feels like a betrayal all the same," Abby whispered, her shoulders trembling. "I trusted him too. Now, I just do not know."

"My heart aches to see you so upset, Milady. I know you feel hurt and betrayed, but things may not be as they seem. My mother always told me that sometimes, the hardest wounds lead to the deepest love," Maude told her.

Abby nodded slowly, the words sinking in like fragile seeds planted in barren soil, never to thrive. More for the maid's sake, she tried to compose herself a little. But all she really wanted was to be alone to nurse her wounds.

Squeezing Maude's hand affectionately, she said, "Thank you, Maude. You are a good friend. I must pull myself together. Would you bring me up some tea? I feel it would do me good. Then I shall have a rest. But I do not wish to see or speak to anyone except you."

"Of course, Milady. I'll fetch the tea right away." Maude rose and left the room.

Abby let out a long sigh, relieved to be alone and give way to the despair inside her. She rose and went to the window, staring sightlessly at the beauty beyond. The same all-consuming grief as when her mother and father had died weighed on her.

She did not see the trees, the lawns, or the flowers. Instead, she saw a bleak future as an old maid, a figure of pity and ridicule, stretching away endlessly before her. And soon, the tears came once more.

* * *

Two days later, in the late afternoon, a distracted Damian was sitting stiffly in the heavy leather armchair opposite Ralph's desk, his fingers drumming absently on the polished wood. On the desk in front of them were stacks of papers—the racing sheets, architectural drawings, and ledgers—the debris of their business meeting. It had been going on since just after luncheon, and Damian prayed it would end soon.

He could hear Ralph talking, but his mind was with Abby. *Her refusal to see me is all my own doing. I should have told her the truth from the start. But now ... it might be too late."*

"Did you hear what I just said?" Ralph asked, breaking into his thoughts.

"Hmm, yes, of course, old chap," he replied, trying to pull himself together and pay attention.

Ralph smiled disbelievingly. "Then you won't mind repeating it back to me, will you?"

Damian gave up pretending. He shrugged. "All right. Sorry, I wasn't listening. I was miles away."

"Thinking about your father?"

No. Your sister.

"Yes, I'm very worried about him," he replied, hating himself for lying to his old friend. *After all, it was lying that got me into this mess in the first place.* But he felt he had no choice. If he could not sort things out with Abby, then the whole future of his and Ralph's joint venture would be in jeopardy, and he had invested heavily. There was a lot at stake if he failed.

Most importantly, my heart. The thought of living without Abby felt like being stabbed in the chest.

"Have you decided to go to home yet?" Ralph asked sympathetically, which made Damian feel even worse.

He sighed. "I don't see I have choice, if he really is at death's door."

"Then go. If you leave instructions about the training program and diet for the new colts, I'm sure we can spare you for a while."

"Thanks, Ralph. I'll probably give it a couple more days before I go. Just to give me time to make sure everything's in place," he hedged.

I need more time to try to persuade your beautiful, stubborn sister to listen to me for a few minutes. That's all I need. My happiness depends up on it.

"Your dedication is noted and will be duly rewarded with a generous measure of claret," Ralph replied. "But unless you want to wheel me over to the sideboard, you'll have to pour it for us."

With a ghost of smile, Damian rose and went to fetch the drinks. "I hope you don't mind if I make mine a large one. I feel I need it." Indeed, he did.

"I hope Abby will be well enough to join us for dinner this evening," Ralph said, frowning as he took the glass of claret Damian handed him. "I don't recall her being ill like this in a long time. It's rather concerning. She seemed so happy at the ball. Perhaps it was too much for her after all."

Damian took a long swallow of claret, worry for Abby gnawing at him. She had not come out of her room since telling him she never wanted to see him again two days ago, pleading illness. She would not receive him nor his increasingly desperate notes pleading to be allowed to talk to her for five minutes, sent via Maude.

"I should at least like to know she's better before I leave," he said.

"Yes, I'm sure she won't like it if you go without saying goodbye."

Oh, my dear friend, you do not know the half of it! Damian thought as he emptied his glass in one go.

Abby did not come down for dinner, increasing his worry and frustration to almost unbearable levels. Damian could not eat, sleep, or think straight. He decided to wait two more days, determined not to give up just yet, hoping she would relent.

Alone in his chambers that evening, he sat down and wrote her a letter. If all his efforts to speak to her failed, he decided to he would leave it for her to read when she was ready. In it, he poured out everything about who he was, the breach with his father, his reasons for covering up his true identity. And his true love for her.

He kept his chamber door open, listening for Maude. As soon as he heard the maid exit Abby's chambers, he intercepted her and gave her the sealed letter.

"Please, Maude. Tell her this is the last I will send. Ask her to read it when she's ready."

Maude gave him a sad smile as she tucked the letter in her apron. "I will, my lord. But I do not know if she will ever read it."

His heart aching, he nodded and retired to his room, feeling suddenly exhausted. He threw himself fully clothed onto the bed and stared up at the bed canopy. He did not see the velvet swagging. All he saw was Abby's face.

* * *

Two days later, shortly after luncheon, Abby stood at a window in one of the front bedrooms, looking down at the drive. She watched as Damian walked out to the hired cab. Before he got in, he turned and looked up at the windows. She stepped back, knowing that if she looked into his eyes, she would be lost.

He looked so downcast when he finally got into the cab, she felt like her heart, already shattered, was breaking all over again.

"He's leaving," she whispered, tears blurring her vision.

A storm of emotions raged within her—sorrow, anger, betrayal. Doubt.

I am doing the right thing by letting him go, she told herself for the hundredth time in the last few tortuous days. She could not fathom why every instinct she possessed was screaming at her to run after him, to hear him out. Why did it feel like she was letting the only chance at happiness she'd ever known walk out of her life?

The door creaked softly behind her, and Maude entered. "Mr. Ross, I mean, Lord Ross, asked me to give you this after he left, Milady." She held out a sealed envelope.

Abby's breath hitched. She glared at the paper as if it had betrayed her personally. Nevertheless, everything in her wanted to snatch it from Maude's hand, tear it open, and read the words he had written for her.

No, I must be strong!

"Burn it, please, Maude. I want nothing more to do with him."

Maude's eyes flickered with sadness. "Are you sure, Milady? He seemed very concerned that you should read it."

Abby looked away, pain lancing through her. "Burn it, I tell you."

"If it pleases you, Milady. I'll take it down to the kitchen and put it in the stove."

Maude tucked the letter back in her apron and left the room. Abby leaned back in her chair and sighed, feeling she would suffocate beneath the weight of her heartbreak.

Chapter Twenty-Three

When Abby finally emerged from her room after days of solitude, her pale face and sunken eyes caused an immediate stir.

Ralph's brows furrowed with concern as he sat opposite her at the breakfast table. "You look washed out, Abby. Are you sure you're recovered enough to be up and about?"

She forced a smile. "Yes. It was just a chill, nothing more. I'll be all right."

Ralph frowned at her. "Well, aren't you supposed to feed a chill? Why don't you try eating some of that toast instead of playing with it?"

"I'm doing my best." She ate a piece of toast the size of a postage stamp.

He rolled his eyes and went back to his eggs. "You know Damian's gone?"

The name was like a spike in her heart. "Yes."

"He had to go home. His father's very ill, you know. Thinks he's on his death bed, apparently."

Shocked, Abby looked up from her plate and stared at him. "I had no idea."

"He didn't tell you?" He looked puzzled.

"No." Abby's stomach was starting to churn. *Was that what he was trying to tell me?*

"I'm surprised, I must say. I thought you two were getting close."

Stunned, she had no response to that.

"Yes, it's a sad story really. He rowed with his father a while back and left home for good. The old man threatened to cut him off, but Damian told him to keep his title and fortune, that he'd earn his own bread by the sweat of his brow. And he's been as good as his word. Fellow of principal, you know. Admirable."

Doubt was creeping over Abby with every word he spoke. "I am confused. What title? What fortune?" she asked, needing confirmation that what she had overheard was correct.

"Didn't he tell you anything?" he asked.

"No."

"Well, that is passing strange. I'm sorry, I imagined he had. Damian is actually the Viscount Amberley, heir to the Earl of Chartringham."

"I see," she replied stiffly. "So, not plain old Mr. Ross then."

"Nope. That was just a precautionary measure to lay low. His father has had men on his trail the whole time, trying to keep tabs on him. If he had used his title, they would have found him easily. You should have seen the look on his face when his father's lawyer turned up here a couple of days ago asking for him. I've seldom seen him so upset."

Despite herself, Abby did not like the thought of Damain hurting, and she was beset by doubts about the way she had treated him. "He has been hiding from his father this whole time?"

"Mmm, poor fellow. He's been pushed out of his home and stands to lose his birthright, and all because of his wicked stepmother."

"Pardon?" Abby said, startled.

"His wicked stepmother, Lady Mariah, his father's second wife. I can't believe he hasn't told you all this already. I know he wanted to speak to you before he left. Was quite adamant about it. But I suppose he never got the chance, what with you being ill and shut up in your chambers."

Abbys' heart slowly sank as Ralph related the sorry tale of Damian's clashes with the high-maintenance Mariah and her defender, his father.

Suddenly, she thought of something. *The letter he left for me. I must read it right away!*

She rose abruptly to her feet. "Excuse me, Brother. I am rather tired and must go and rest." Without waiting for his answer, she hurried from the room and ran upstairs to her chambers.

Maude was there, turning the bed down when she rushed in.

"Maude, where is that letter Mr. Ross, I mean, Lord Ross, left for me?" she panted to the startled maid.

"You told me to burn it, Milady," the maid answered.

Overcome by dizziness, thinking she was about to swoon, Abby put a hand on the door frame to steady herself. *Then all really is lost!*

"But I disobeyed your orders, Milady," Maude said, smiling tentatively as she pulled the letter from her apron pocket and handed it to Abby.

Recovering quickly as excitement took the place of sorrow, Abby took it with trembling hand, hope burgeoning in her chest.

"Oh, Maude! You are an angel. Your disobedience shall be rewarded," she said breathlessly, reaching for the letter knife and slitting the letter open.

My dearest Abby,

Forgive me the presumption of writing, when you have made so plain your wish not to see me again. But I can no longer remain unheard. You deserve the truth—all of it—and though I fear it may be too late to win back even a shred of your trust, I must try.

I never meant to deceive you. That is the first thing I must say. When I introduced myself to you as Mr. Ross, it was not with the intent to manipulate or conceal out of vanity or pride. It was self-preservation, plain and simple. I concealed my noble background not to hide from the world, but from the man who made it impossible for me to wear it with honor—my father, the Earl of Chartringham.

Eighteen months ago, after countless attempts to speak reason, I could no longer abide his blind indulgence of my stepmother Lady Mariah's schemes. Her hunger for wealth, her whispered lies, her games—I will not sully this letter with the details. But know this: I could not remain under that roof another day. I left with nothing but the clothes on my back and the one talent I knew to be truly mine—my way with horses.

I became Mr. Ross not to trick you, but because I needed to become someone who was not hunted by his title or shackled by the sins of his family. In truth, I had almost forgotten I wasn't plain Mr. Ross.

When I came to Worsley, I did not expect to find true love. I did not even believe in it. My opinion of marriage being low, I had vowed never to wed.

But then I met you, and everything changed. I have changed. With you, I have known the first true happiness of my life. And to find that you—you—looked on me with similar affection too? It undid me completely.

I should have told you everything sooner. I meant to—God knows I did. But you must admit that, in keeping me at arm's length for so long, you did not make it easy to grow trust and share confidences.

But after the ball and what we shared in the garden, I was the happiest man alive. I was overjoyed to have your sacred trust. I should have told you everything about myself there and then, but I was so swept up in my feelings, I failed to do so.

No one can regret that delay more than I. Because of it, I fear I have lost you forever.

Abby, I would give anything—my title, my inheritance, every acre of Chartringham—if only I could undo the hurt I caused you. You told me you could never trust me again, and I understand it. I do. But I beg you to believe that my feelings for you have never been false. They are the truest thing I have ever known.

I love you.

There it is, in ink at last. I love you with every part of myself. I love the way you laugh when you think no one is watching, the fire in your eyes when you argue about things that matter, the gentleness with which you speak to even the smallest creature. I love you as I never believed I could love anyone.

I wish to marry you. Not to possess you, but to honor and cherish you. If you can ever find it in your heart to forgive me, I swear to spend the rest of my days striving to earn the trust I lost and to prove my love for you is no fleeting thing.

If this letter brings only pain, then burn it. But if there is even the faintest ember of what once was between us, I beg you, let it live. Let us not throw away what we had before it even has a chance to blossom.

Yours in truth and devotion,

Damian

As the words sank in, Abby's head swam. The letter fell from her trembling hand to the floor.

* * *

The following morning, Abby sat across from Claire in the front parlor of the vicarage, a tray of tea between them on a low table. She bit her lip as she nervously waited for Claire to finish reading the letter.

"What passion in his words," her friend declared feelingly, folding the sheets carefully and handing them back to Abby. "I quite feel as though I am a character in a romantic novel. Mr. Fielding never wrote me anything like this. I am rather jealous. His explanation for misleading you is very clear, and he apologizes for it. Why did you wait so long before reading his letter? It would have saved you a lot of heartache."

"You know why. I was angry with him for his betrayal of my trust. Part of me still is. But I love him still. I cannot seem to stop. And I do not know what to do now."

"Well, is it so hard to decide? He loves you. You love him. Problem solved. All you have to do is write to him and explain your delay in replying. Tell him you forgive him. That you return his feelings."

Abby hesitated, torn between hope and fear. "What if he's angry? What if he no longer cares for me?"

Claire smiled gently. "True love does not simply evaporate in the space of a few weeks, I think. Write to him, Abby. You have nothing to lose and everything to gain by reaching out to him."

* * *

Charles Ross, the Earl of Chartringham's chambers smelled of medicine and stale air, of lingering sickness. Outside, it was a fine June day. Inside the room, a fire burned in the grate. Damian, sweating beneath his coat, steeled himself as he approached the enormous four-poster bed, and the frail figure that lay beneath the covers.

His heart clenched in shock when he looked down on the pale, emaciated face of his father lying on the pillow. He hardly recognized it. The old man's eyes were closed, and in his vulnerable state, looked to have aged twenty years since Damian had seen him last.

He was hale and hearty when I left. What illness has laid him low like this?

"Father, are you awake? It's me, Damian," he murmured, slipping into the chair next to the bed, clasping one of his father's hands in his as he leaned over him.

His father's eyes flickered open. He turned his head and fixed his son with a dull, glassy gaze. "Damian. You've come at last. Thank God," he croaked, his dry lips stretching into a semblance of a smile. "So, they tracked you down at last, eh? Took them long enough."

Damian's anger at being found was fading fast. He had no heart to berate his father about it. Not now he had seen for himself how ill he was.

"It would seem so, yes. What is this illness, Father? How long have you been like this? What does the physician say?"

"A lot of rot. I've been like this on and off now since Christmastide, and none of the doctors seem to know what's wrong with me or how to cure it. I had to write, dear boy. I was worried I'd turn my toes up before we had a chance to reconcile. Couldn't leave it like that between us."

"Six months?" Damian said, shocked and beset by guilt for his stubborn pride in allowing this to happen through his absence. "Then I shall find better doctors. What are the symptoms you have been suffering?"

"It is my digestion. I eat, and I have an attack. I don't eat, and I grow weaker. I am tired." He clutched his son's hand and looked in his eyes. "I have to tell you, Son, not a day has gone by since you left that I have not regretted our falling out. I can admit now, you were right about many things. I have made mistakes."

"What do you mean, Father? What was I right about? What mistakes?" He knew very well what his father was referring to, but he wanted him to say it.

The Earl closed his eyes briefly. "About Mariah."

"I see. And when did you finally realize this?" Damian felt no gratification for being right, only sorrow at seeing this strong man brought so low by that scheming vixen.

"Oh, not long after you left, with it just being the two of us, I started to notice things. Things I had turned a blind eye to before ... because I suppose I did not want to see them."

"So, she's still stealing off you then?"

"Yes, and she's very skilled at covering it up. But not as skilled as my bankers are in finding discrepancies with the accounting. They spotted that my signature has been forged on several bank drafts, which enabled her to withdraw quite large sums, it seems."

He gave a crackling, mirthless laugh. "To think a slip of a woman a has been pulling the wool over my eyes for so long. You called me an old fool. You were never more right, Son. I am truly sorry for not listening to you in the first place."

"I'm truly sorry too, Father. It gives me no pleasure to be proved right. Is there anything left of the family fortune, or has she spent it all?"

"Thankfully, she only had access to my general account. The rest of it, the investments and so on, she couldn't touch any of that. But I'm sure she plans to get her hands on it very soon. On everything, in fact. Unless she's stopped."

He spoke in such an odd way, Damian was driven to ask, "What do you mean?"

They were briefly interrupted when a maid arrived. "Milady has sent up a slice of almond tart for you, Milord, which she hopes will encourage your appetite," she said, setting a tray down on the nightstand before leaving.

Damian was surprised at Mariah's unexpected kindness. Yet he noticed how his father looked at the tart with distaste, and a flicker of fear in his eyes.

"Would you like some tart, Father?" he asked, thinking he must be mistaken.

The old earl shook his head weakly. "No. And I strongly advise you not to eat it either nor feed it to any other living thing. Take it with you when you go and dispose of it in the privy."

"What?" Damian asked, starting to suspect the old man was turning senile. But that idea was dispelled by his father's next words.

"Poison, dear boy. I think my wife is trying to kill me."

Chapter Twenty-Four

As if his seat had turned to hot coals, Damian sprang out of his chair and stared at his father in disbelief.

"You believe Mariah is trying to poison you?" he asked, finding the idea far-fetched. *But it is not impossible. Especially knowing Mariah.*

"I believe it, but as yet, I have no proof," his father replied.

"This is a serious accusation, Father. What grounds do you have for making it? When did you start to suspect?"

"I came to the conclusion only recently. There were too many times when Madam's fortifying soups and broths and such like were followed by an attack, each one more severe than the last."

"But— but why did you not put a stop to it?" Damain asked, horrified and furious.

The earl gave his skull-like smile. "No proof."

"Have you told anyone about this? This needs to be thoroughly investigated at once."

"I have told no one of my suspicions except you and Hayworth."

Hayworth was the butler who had served their family faithfully since before Damian was born. His loyalty was unquestioned.

"I tasked him with finding out how she is putting the poison in my food and drink. It seems that Madam has a habit of checking whatever is prepared for me before the maid brings it up. We think that is when she does it. My hypothesis of poison is supported by the fact that since Hayworth has been in charge of everything I consume, I have shown a marked improvement."

Damian could only speculate as to what state the old man had been in before Hayworth's interceptions. He looked to be at death's door now.

"I know what you are thinking. I look like a corpse. However, I am feeling better, but it would be too dangerous to let Madam know that in case she suspects we are on to her."

"Good Lord, this is outrageous, beyond belief," Damian raged quietly, his fists clenching.

"By the time I realized what she is most likely doing, she had already managed to isolate me from you and everyone. Visitors are turned away, my correspondence is vetted. She long ago dispensed with Dr. Clarke's services and sends physicians of her own choosing. She controls it all, and now I am now too weak to challenge her. I fear that if I do, I shall soon succumb to this mysterious "illness" of mine. That is why I had to find you and bring you home, Son. You alone can put a stop to it."

There was a heavy pause while each contemplated the other.

"I am astonished, Father. Never in my wildest imagining could I have foreseen such a scenario. She is beyond evil," Damian finally said, hardly able to take it all in. It was not at all what he had expected of the homecoming.

"I know I have been foolish, Damian. But I pray you can forgive me for my mistakes enough to help me now," the old earl said, his grip tightening on Damian's hand, a flicker of hope in his eyes.

"None of that seems important now, Father. Thank God you found me and called me home. You no longer need to worry about anything but getting well. I will see to everything."

The Earl's smile reappeared, tinged with relief. "Thank you, Son."

"But you must give me the power to act on your behalf. I must have control of everything."

"You have it."

"And I have your permission to act as I see fit to remedy the situation?"

"You have that too. But at the same time, remember our reputation must be protected. If Mariah is shown in public for what she truly is, it will reflect badly on all of us. I trust you will handle her with the appropriate discretion, or she could be very troublesome to us in the future."

Damian rose to his feet, his resolve fixed. He would cut out the canker that had been consuming his father and their family for too long once and for all.

"Don't worry, Father, you can trust me to deal with her without causing a scandal. I won't let you down."

The skull smiled again, and the bony hand gripped his. "I knew I could rely on you, Son."

* * *

It had taken hours of careful thought and many abandoned attempts before Abby was satisfied with the letter she had written in reply to Damian's. But she was mindful that six weeks had passed since he had left it for her.

Am I too late?

The finished letter was in her reticule now, safe from the teeming rain that had started just as she left the hall and begun her walk to the village post office. She wanted to post the letter herself and be sure it was on its way.

Her umbrella protected her top half from the worst of the rain as she walked along the lane, oblivious to the muddy puddles splashing the hem of her gown. She was too preoccupied to notice. Her mind was on her letter. Had she worded it right? Had she made her feelings clear enough? Would Damian understand or care that she loved him still?

As she walked, she mouthed the lines she had so carefully composed, knowing them almost by heart, imagining him reading them.

My dear Damian,

I scarcely know how to begin.

Your letter has left me quite undone. I have read it more times than I care to admit, each reading softening something in me I thought had hardened forever. I do not deserve the kindness of your words, nor the depth of feeling you have offered so freely after all I said in anger.

I was hurt. That much, you already know. But what I did not allow myself to see—what I see so clearly now—was how much you were hurting too. I mistook silence for deception and caution for betrayal. I heard only the name you had not given me, and not the truth of the man who stood before me every day, honest in his affection, generous in his attentions, and entirely himself.

You never pretended to be more than you were. It was I who assumed you less.

If I could take back the things I said that morning, I would do so a thousand times over. I spoke from pain, yes—but also from pride, and that was my failing. I thought I was protecting myself from heartbreak, when in truth I was only closing the door on the very thing my heart has long desired.

I forgive you. Freely, and without condition.

And more than that—I must ask your forgiveness in turn. I judged too swiftly, loved too fearfully, and in doing so, I nearly lost the one man who has ever truly known me.

You wrote that you love me. I have read those words so many times I know them by heart. And so now, let me answer in kind:

I love you, Damian. Not for your title, nor your lineage, nor the estate that may one day be yours—but for the man who pulled me from the lake when I was drowning, who saved Alba, who loves horses. The man who saw me when others merely looked. The man who kissed my scars.

If it is not too late, then I hope—I pray—that we may begin again. Write to me or come to me when you can. My heart is open to you alone.

Yours,

In hope and love,

Abby

She was at the post box now. Balancing her umbrella in the crook of her arm, she opened her reticule and took out the letter. First making sure no one was watching, she kissed the envelope, breathing in the rose perfume she had sprinkled on it.

"You hold all my hope and prayers. Do not let me down," she told it before popping it into the mailbox. She stared at the dark opening for a moment before finally turning back the way she had come.

For the first time in six long weeks of misery, she felt a flicker of optimism in her heart.

* * *

"What is all that commotion going on out there?" asked Lady Mariah Ross, her pretty nose wrinkling with annoyance. "Go and look, will you?"

"Yes, Milady." The maid bobbed a curtsey and obediently went to peek out of the door of the mistress' private sitting room into the hall.

"Well, what is it, girl?" the countess asked querulously, stirring her hot chocolate.

"I'm not sure, Milady, but Master Damian is there with Mr. Hayworth, and two of the footmen are carrying a painting into the yellow drawing room by the looks of it."

The countess' elegantly arched brows shot up. "What painting? No one has consulted me about any painting. We shall see about this. How dare he!" Red spots appeared on her powdered cheeks as she rose to her feet and glided to the door. The well-schooled maid was already holding it open for her.

"Would you mind explaining to me what exactly is going on here?" she asked her stepson with acid politeness when she joined him on the threshold of the yellow drawing room.

"I am putting my mother's portrait back where it belongs," Damian replied, his handsome features, which she had once found so mesmerizing, cold as granite.

Seething, she turned to Hayworth. "You may leave us, for the moment, Hayworth," she told the butler imperiously. "All of you."

"Milady," Hayworth intoned with a bow before directing the footmen to carefully lean the portrait against the wall and then quickly vanishing with them below stairs.

As soon as they had gone, Mariah turned on Damian, letting her anger show. "Do I have to remind you that this is my house? You have no right to come here and move things about willy-nilly as you please. I moved that painting for a good reason."

"And what, pray, would that be?" Scorn burned in his eyes as he looked down on her.

He had always looked down on her since the first time she had entered the house, when Charles had introduced her as his betrothed. She could still remember how the blood had drained from Damian's face. The most beautiful face a man could ever possess. Even in that moment, she had wondered how she could ditch the father in order to get to the son.

Alas, her overtures had all been coldly rejected. And her unrequited passion had turned to hate. To an insatiable need for revenge.

She pulled herself up to her full height. "I designed the new décor for the yellow drawing room myself. The portrait did not suit the color palette. It had to be moved."

"To the east wing?" he asked bitingly. "Where no one ever goes."

"Yes, why not?" she retorted defiantly, chin held high. "I have been mistress of this house for four years. Whereas your mother is long dead. Even your father has forgotten her. What harm is there in moving that dreadfully out-of-date painting to a quieter spot?"

The words were meant to wound, and she saw with satisfaction how he bristled at her mention of his mother. She wanted to provoke him into a fight. Then, her tears would easily persuade Charles to send him packing.

His sudden reappearance after nearly two years had almost had her fainting. And when she inquired what had brought him back, he had said, "I heard Father was ill." But how had he heard when she controlled all the post that went in and out of the house? Her suspicions were on Hayworth, and she was making sure the traitorous old butler felt her wrath daily.

To her disappointment, he only said coolly, "Be careful what you say when you speak of my mother. She deserves respect. Even yours. You may be mistress of this house now, but you never know when that may change."

Taken aback, she nonetheless laughed. "Is that supposed to be a threat?"

"It is not a threat. It is, let's say, a premonition."

"Ah! You are thinking that as soon as your father dies—and the doctors all say he is fading fast—this will all be yours." She swept her arm about the hall, but her gesture implied the totality of his inheritance.

"But your father knows what you are like, and he has made plentiful provision for me to guard against your spite after his death. Chartringham will be my home until I die. How pleasant that will be, for us to reside beneath the same roof, do you not think?"

Irritatingly, he ignored her barbs and strode into the drawing room to tug on the bell rope.

"What are you doing?" she demanded, frustrated. He was not rising to her bait as he should.

"I am ringing for assistance."

"You still mean to put that portrait in my drawing room?"

"I think you will find it is my drawing room. And yes, I do." Hayworth and the footmen reappeared. "Take down the one down that's over the mantel now and hang this in its place," he ordered them. The men prepared to do as he asked.

"Wait!" she barked, stopping them in their tracks. "The portrait hanging over the hearth is one your father commissioned especially, to commemorate our wedding. I forbid you to remove it."

She was horribly conscious of the servants watching everything.

"It will look better in the blue drawing room," Damian said, gesturing for the footmen to go ahead. They picked up the huge painting and carried it inside the room. "It will go with the color palette there more effectively, I believe."

"We shall see what your father has to say about this," she said, making for the stairs in a flurry of skirts.

"Oh, I have not had a chance to tell you yet. You are banned from entering his room from now on. In fact, you will not try to see him or speak to him again."

Astonished, she stopped and stared back at him. "Have you lost your mind? He is my husband. I will see him whenever I choose." She started up the staircase.

"Madam, you will not." His deep voice cut through the air so commandingly, she stopped. "You will do as I say. Father has granted me the power to act on his behalf in all things pertaining to this family. That includes you."

Mariah tried to hide her shock, yet inside, she was reeling. "You cannot keep me from him. He will want to see me. He needs me."

"I assure you, Madam, he does not wish to see you ever again. You will also have no hand in his care from this time forward. I shall oversee his victuals and his medical needs."

From where she was standing, she could see the men taking down the painting of her and Charles, and she knew they could hear everything. Over and above that, she scented danger.

He knows about the poison.

Slowly, she turned and started down the stairs. "Perhaps we could have a quiet word in the earl's study?" she asked Damian sweetly, wishing she could plunge a blade into his heart.

"As you wish." He led the way to the study and allowed her to enter before following her and shutting the door.

Chapter Twenty-Five

"Well, she's gone," he told his father an hour later.

"Yes. Didn't exactly go quietly, did she?" the old man asked. He was in his silk banyan, a skeleton looking out his chamber window.

"No, she most certainly did not. But she's on her way to a hotel for the night, and then tomorrow, she'll take up permanent residence at the house I have purchased for her in Kensington. She won't be troubling us again, Father. I have made sure of it."

The Earl turned and smiled at him, relief and affection in his eyes. "Thank you, Son. For saving my life. And for putting up with a stubborn, foolish old man for so long."

"No apology needed, Father. I have to confess it was a pleasure to see the look on her face when I showed her those bank drafts with the forged signatures."

"She tried to deny it, I expect."

"Naturally. But when I offered to have the constables look into it, she agreed to all the terms I had laid out for her. Really, she has nothing to complain of. You have given her a handsome annual allowance, and as long as she never darkens our door again, she should be content."

"Did she admit to poisoning me?"

"No. It was unnecessary to raise the issue. I would not expect her to admit it anyway. She would hang if it could be proved. But she's too clever for that."

"Do you know, Son, I feel like a weight's been lifted off me. In fact, I feel rather peckish. Shall we ring for some tea?"

Damian smiled as he pulled the bell rope, glad to see his father snapping back to his old self so quickly. He would forever be thankful that he had heeded his call and returned to Chartringham just in time.

Refreshments were brought, and the pair sat together over a small table, as they had often used to do before Mariah came between them. With matters at home settled, Damian's thoughts turned back to the other burning issue on his mind.

"Father?"

"Hmm?"

"I have met a lady I intend to propose to."

The old man's emaciated features lit up like a lantern. "Well, that's splendid news, my boy. I had been wondering if you would ever settle down."

"I said I intend to propose to her. I haven't done it yet. There's no guarantee she'll say yes."

"Pshaw! Of course she will. Unless she's a fool. And if she's your chosen one, I doubt that."

"Well, it's not so simple as that." Damian said, and then he proceeded to tell his father all that had occurred between him and Abby.

"That is very unfortunate, and I am sorry for your pain, Son. Love is such a funny thing. It brings joy, but it can equally bring heartache. But you say you're going to propose anyway?"

"I have nothing more to lose."

"Then why are you sitting here with me, you dunderhead? You're wasting valuable time. Go and see her at once."

Damian stared at him in disbelief. "Father, you are just coming back from the brink of death. I am hardly going to leave you now."

"Oh, no, you're not getting out of it like that. Hayworth is more than capable of handling things here, and I have a whole army of servants to look after me. If you do not leave and go and speak to your lady at once, we shall fall out again. I insist you go."

A grin formed on Damian's lips. This was the father he loved and respected, returned to him.

"Are you sure?" he asked.

"Sure as eggs, dear boy. I want to meet my new daughter-in-law as soon as possible. I want plenty of grandchildren, too, so hurry up and see about it."

"Her name is Lady Abigail Lucas. Her father was Lord Richard Lucas, Baron of Harkness. She lives in Buckinghamshire."

"Ah. That makes sense. Garland told me you were living at Lord Lucas' home. She's his sister. Worsley House, is it? Take my carriage, Son. It'll be quicker that way."

"Is there anything you don't know about me, Father?" Damian asked with a happy sigh.

"Very little, Son. Very little."

He arrived at Worsley two days later, in the middle of a balmy afternoon. Withers greeted him with pleasure, and when Damian inquired, informed him that the Master was in his study.

He knocked, heard Ralph's grunt, and pushed open the door.

"Damian, old fellow. What a delight to see you. You have been sorely missed," Ralph rose grinning from the chair behind his desk. Grabbing a walking stick, he hobbled over to embrace his friend.

"How's your father?" Ralph asked.

"Much better. And the dragon has been banished."

"Oh? Well, that's excellent news. I'm very happy for you. You can fill me in on all the gory details at dinner. You are back and staying for dinner, I take it?"

"It depends."

"On what?"

"On what your sister says when I ask her to marry me."

There was a moment of stunned silence as Ralph stared at him. Damian felt a frisson of fear, wondering if Ralph was going to object.

But then his face split into a grin, and he began laughing. "Well, thank goodness for that! You certainly took your time getting around to it, old man. I've been waiting for you to do something. I have no idea what went on between you, but she's been so down in the dumps since you left, I really started to worry. Almost wrote to you myself to ask you to come back."

Hope kindled in Damian's breast. "She's been sad? As if she's been missing me?"

"Well, I'm no real judge when it comes to women and their feelings, but I'd bet good money on it, yes."

Damian could hardly contain his joy. "You have no objection to me marrying her then? If she accepts that is, which is by no means certain."

"On the contrary, I'm delighted. Think of how convenient it will be to run the business with you two as man and wife."

"Thanks, Ralph. You're a gentleman of the first water and a scholar to boot."

"I know. Now, I think you've wasted enough time. She's out riding somewhere. Off you go and find her. Shoo!" He waved his fingers at the door. "And don't come back until the deed is done. While you're gone, I'll have Withers put some champagne on ice."

"Isn't that a bit premature? What if she turns me down?"

Ralph laughed again. "Off you go, out, out!"

"All right if I take Warrior?" Damian asked, already heading for the door, figuring the great stallion would get him to Abby all the faster.

"If you don't mess things up, we'll soon to be brothers. What's mine is yours. Now, buzz off."

His fragile hopes bolstered by Ralph's confidence in his success, Damian left without further ado and set out for the stables.

* * *

Abby raced over the gallops, urging Silver forward with her heels, remembering all the times when she and Damian had done the same, riding side by side, laughing as they flew over the turf.

But that is all gone now. I have lost him. Through my own fear and stubbornness.

She slowed Silver, the brief moment of forgetfulness the speed had provided ended, and bleak reality came crashing in once more.

Ten days had passed since she posted the letter, and still she had received no response from Damian. With each day that passed with no word, she resigned herself a little more to never again seeing the man she loved. To being a lonely, scarred old maid.

By the burnt oak, she reined in and slid from the saddle onto the grass. She let Silver wander while she leaned on the fence and looked at the jagged old tree etched against the azure sky.

The world surrounding her was undeniably beautiful, full of sunshine and birdsong. But the hole where her heart used to be was cold and ached like a hollow tooth.

I will never get over him. I will never be truly happy again.

Behind her, Silver nickered. Abby turned to look at him. The dappled horse pranced and swished his tail as if excited by something. But there was nothing for miles. "What is it, Silver?" she asked curiously.

The she heard it. It was faint at first. But as the sound grew louder, it was unmistakable. Thundering hooves.

"Someone is coming, yes," she told the horse. "I expect it is Michael or Billy, exercising one of your friends. Is that what you are so excited about, you silly thing?"

The horse whinnied and kicked up his heels, acting so strangely that Abby looked down the gallops, shielding her eyes from the sun with her hand.

Nothing. But then, from around the curve, a rider appeared, racing towards her. It was Warrior. But she could not make out who was riding him. Whoever it was, they were approaching fast.

As the horse and rider drew nearer, details came into focus. She saw a long duster coat flying out behind, dark hair blowing in the breeze.

Her heart began racing too, at top speed.

"It cannot be. It is! Damian!"

She dropped her riding crop and began running towards him.

As he reached her, he reigned in sharply and leapt from the saddle. Letting Warrior go, he ran the rest of the way to meet her.

They stopped a few feet away from each other, both panting, eyes locked.

"Damian. Is it really you?" she asked, staring at him in wonder, her heart going wild.

"Yes, Abby, it's me. Turning up like a bad penny," he said, giving her the lovely, warm smile she had missed so much and never thought to see again.

"You got my letter then? I posted it myself ten days ago."

He frowned and shook his head. "No, I haven't had any letter. But that is perhaps unsurprising, what with the rain we've been having, the roads are pretty terrible. I expect it's been held up somewhere."

Her spirits fell. "Oh."

"Why? What was in it?" he asked curiously, stepping closer.

"Never mind. How is your father? I was sorry to hear he was ill."

"He's on the road to recovery, thank you. Abby, what was in your letter?"

"You really want to know?"

He quirked an eyebrow.

"It said ... I wrote ... some things ..."

"Yes." He took a step closer. She thought her heart was about to explode.

She took a deep breath, figuring she had nothing to lose. "That were very similar in sentiment to the things you wrote in your last letter to me."

The way his face lit up with joy as he grasped her around the waist and whirled her around and around told her all she needed to know.

After he set her back on her feet, keeping her close within the circle of his arms, they could not seem to talk fast enough. Words pent-up for weeks came tumbling from their mouths: explanations, apologies, words of forgiveness. And, finally, declarations of love.

Damian gave her so much joy, but never more than when he suddenly dropped to his knee before her, took her hand in his, and said, "Abby, would you do me the honor of becoming by wife?"

She hesitated to answer, not because she had doubts, but because she had never thought she would hear anyone ask her that question, especially not the beautiful, handsome man in front of her, the man she thought she had lost, who held her heart in his hand.

"Yes, Damian," she breathed after a moment, gazing down into those beautiful green eyes so full of love. "Yes, yes, yes!"

Epilogue

The morning sun shone soft and golden upon the chapel at Chartringham as if the heavens themselves had conspired to smile upon the day. White rose petals, gathered from the gardens, lay scattered along the chapel path, and soft strains of Handel floated from within. Plying the organ keys was Claire's now-official fiancé, her father's sexton, the formerly hard-to-pin-down Mr. Fielding.

His betrothed, in her best hat and beaming from ear to ear, was sitting in the second row of pews. The rest were filled with close friends and family, all gathered to witness the marriage of Lady Abigail Lucas to Lord Damian Ross, the Viscount Amberley.

Seated in the Ross family box pew at the front was Lord Charles Ross, the Earl of Chartringham, looking proud as punch. Damian was overjoyed that his father had returned to full health. He had filled out again, and the color had returned to his cheeks. Besides that, without Mariah around, he seemed more cheerful, like his old self.

In the other box pew, sitting with her parents among a selection of aunts, was Caroline, now Ralph's betrothed. The couple had set a date in a month's time for their wedding.

Damian stood nervously before the altar, the sunlight gilding the edge of his dark hair, hands clasped behind his back. His coat was impeccably tailored in a shade of deep navy that set off his green eyes. He was quite pleased with his appearance and hoped Abby would feel the same.

Though, earlier that morning, Lyle, as best man and supportive best friend, had pronounced him to be merely "not quite as repulsively ugly as usual"—before promptly adjusting his own cravat with a grin.

Damian inhaled sharply at the sound of the chapel doors creaking open. He glanced around at Lyle, who winked at him and mouthed, "She's coming."

Is it all right to look? I'm going to look.

He looked, and his breath left his body.

Abby, radiant in ivory lace, her auburn hair caught up in an elegant coil beneath a veil fastened with delicate pearls, was walking beside her brother, holding his arm with grace and poise, though Damian noted the slight tremor of her fingers.

Her eyes—bright silver—met his. The chapel, the guests, the quiet gasp of someone moved to tears—it all melted away. There was only her.

"You are," he murmured when she reached him, his voice low, reverent, "utterly magnificent."

Abby's lips curved. "Let us see if you say the same when I've spilt wine on your fine wedding breeches this evening."

He smiled and offered his hand, which she took without hesitation.

Reverend Potter opened his Bible and began the service.

The ceremony unfolded with grace and simplicity, the words of union spoken with solemn joy. Abby's voice caught briefly when she began her vows, but Damian's steady hand calmed her. When she said, "I will," the promise rang like a quiet bell in his chest.

With the kiss that sealed their vows, a joyful flutter stirred through the chapel, and Caroline was heard to sniffle and whisper to her intended, "Oh, Ralph, wasn't it perfect?"

Outside, the newlyweds emerged into a burst of rose petals and laughter. Waiting for them at the foot of the chapel steps was a gleaming curricle, its harness adorned with white ribbon. Hitched at the front, as if summoned from legend, stood Alba alongside Silver, the horses' coats gleaming, manes plaited, their harnesses decked with silver bells.

Abby gasped and clutched Damian's arm. "Oh, what a lovely surprise! They look wonderful, don't they?"

Damin smirked. "I thought you'd appreciate that," he said, helping her up into the seat.

Their guests waved and cheered as Alba and Silver trotted them back along the shaded lane to the main house, their carefully combed tails whisking with equine pride.

"You've made my whole life feel like a fairytale," Abby told Damian as they turned the final corner.

He reached for her hand. "No, my love. This is the start of a very real one. And you, the bravest, most beautiful heroine in it."

She melted into his arms. "I love you, Husband."

"How very convenient that we are married then, Wife," he said, smiling as he kissed the top of her head. "Because I love you too."

THE END

Thank you for reading "The Earl to be In Disguise."

If you liked the story PLEASE Leave a review

https://www.amazon.com/review/create-review?&asin=B0FKNHBTDK

Every review truly makes a difference. As an indie author, I rely on readers like you to help my stories find their way into more hearts.

If you enjoyed this Regency romance, would you consider leaving a short review?
Just a few words can help another reader decide to take the leap—and it means the world to me personally.

You can leave your review here:

https://www.amazon.com/review/create-review?&asin=B0FKNHBTDK

**Thank you so much for being part of this journey.
With gratitude,
Kerri Kastle**

If you loved this book, then you will love "Clara, Stitched in Secrets"

Click here and get your copy of "Clara Stitched in Secrets" https://www.amazon.com/dp/B0D8RHB95B

SNEAK PEEK of Clara Stitched in Secrets:

Chapter One

Clara Mills had done many questionable things in her twenty-two years of life, but sneaking into a grand ball through the servants' entrance while wearing a stolen—*borrowed*, she corrected herself—mask definitely topped the list.

Her heart thundered against her ribs as she slipped through the back door of Pembroke House, careful not to snag her midnight blue gown on the rough wooden frame.

The dress was another one of her "borrowed" items for the night, rescued from a client who'd deemed it unfashionable after one wearing.

Clara had spent three nights transforming it, and now no one would recognize the once-plain gown with its newly added silver embroidery and delicate beading.

Just like no one recognizes the seamstress behind Madame Celestine's creations, she thought with a mixture of pride and irritation.

The mask she wore—a masterpiece of silver filigree and blue silk that had cost her three sleepless nights to perfect—felt both like armor and a prison.

Protection from discovery, yes, but also a constant reminder that she didn't belong in this glittering world she'd been skirting for the past five years.

Fix Lady Pembroke's dress and leave, she reminded herself firmly. *No lingering, no dreaming, no—*

"Watch where you're going!" A harried footman nearly collided with her, his arms full of fresh flowers.

Clara pressed herself against the wall, inhaling the mingled scents of beeswax candles, roses, and excitement that always seemed to perfume these grand events. So different from the lavender and cotton that scented her tiny shop in the unfashionable part of London.

Her fingers tightened around her sewing kit—the same battered leather case she'd had since she was sixteen. Back then, she'd been nothing but a seamstress's apprentice with callused fingers and impossible dreams.

Now she was... well, still a seamstress with callused fingers, but one whose creations graced the finest ballrooms in London. Even if she had to pretend to be French to make it happen.

The servants' corridors buzzed with pre-ball chaos. Maids rushed past with trays of champagne, footmen hauled ice sculptures, and somewhere nearby a butler was having what sounded like an absolute fit about the wrong vintage being served.

Clara navigated through it all with the ease of someone who'd spent more time below stairs than above them.

Five years, she mused, ducking into an alcove to let a line of footmen pass.

Five years since she'd first had the mad idea to reinvent herself as the mysterious Madame Celestine. She'd been seventeen, desperate, and tired of watching her designs being claimed by her employer.

The French accent had been an impulsive addition—after all, who would trust an English girl barely out of her teens with their finest gowns?

But it had worked. Oh, how it had worked.

"Madame Celestine!" Lady Pembroke's urgent whisper cut through her reminiscing. "Thank heavens you've come!"

Clara turned to find her latest client half-hidden in a side chamber, clutching what appeared to be a significant amount of torn silk.

Right then. Time to work some magic.

She squared her shoulders, adjusted her mask one final time, and glided forward with all the confidence of her alter ego. Time to be the miracle worker they all believed Madame Celestine to be.

Even if her hands were shaking slightly within her gloves.

Lady Pembroke yanked Clara into the side chamber with surprising strength for someone wearing what appeared to be half the silk in London. "Look at this disaster!"

Clara assessed the damage with practiced eyes.

The tear in the cornflower blue silk was substantial—running a good six inches along the side seam—but nothing she couldn't fix. She'd repaired worse damage in less time, usually while some society lady wept dramatically nearby.

"How did this happen?" Clara asked, already reaching for her needle and thread.

"That horrible little dog of Lady Ashworth's! The beast caught my skirts as I was coming down the stairs and—" Lady Pembroke made a ripping gesture that sent her bracelets jangling.

Clara bit back a smile.

She'd met Lady Ashworth's "horrible little dog"—a perfectly sweet creature who probably just wanted attention. Much like its owner.

As she worked, her quick fingers weaving invisible stitches through the delicate silk, fragments of conversation drifted in from the hallway.

"Can you believe Eustace Montague actually came?"

"The Duke hasn't attended a ball in months..."

"Still brooding over that Italian fiancée..."

Clara's hands never paused, but her ears pricked up.

Everyone knew about the Duke of Ravencroft and his broken engagement—it had been last season's favorite scandal. She'd heard all about it while fitting gowns for gossiping ladies.

Poor man, she thought, then immediately corrected herself. *Poor rich, handsome duke with his enormous estate and broken heart. However does he manage?*

"Stand still, my lady," she murmured as Lady Pembroke fidgeted. "Just one more minute."

Working quickly but carefully—because rushed stitches were obvious stitches, as her first teacher had drilled into her head—Clara finished the repair. She sat back on her heels, surveying her work with critical eyes.

Perfect. Not even she could spot where the tear had been.

"There," she said, knotting the final stitch. "Good as new."

Lady Pembroke twisted to examine the repair in a nearby mirror. "Magnificent! You truly are a miracle worker, Madame Celestine." She clasped Clara's hands. "You simply must join the ball as my guest. I insist!"

Say no, her sensible side urged. *Get out while you can.*

But through the chamber's window, Clara caught a glimpse of the gardens. Moonlight silvered the paths and turned the fountain's spray to diamonds. Music drifted in—a waltz, her favorite. And for just a moment, she allowed herself to imagine...

Don't you dare, the practical voice in her head warned. *Remember what happened last time you got carried away with dreams?*

She should leave. She had three gowns to finish, a rent payment due, and absolutely no business pretending to be anything other than what she was—a working woman with a gift for needle and thread.

But oh, how beautiful it all looked. Just one small taste of the world she spent her life adorning others for...

"You're already dressed for it," Lady Pembroke coaxed, gesturing to Clara's gown. "And that mask is simply divine. Your own work, I assume?"

Clara touched the mask self-consciously. Three nights of work, yes, but worth every pricked finger and lost hour of sleep. The silver filigree caught the light just so, and the blue silk perfectly matched her eyes—not that anyone would see them behind the mask.

"Just for a moment," she whispered, more to herself than to Lady Pembroke. "What's the worst that could happen?"

Five years of careful planning, of building her reputation stitch by stitch, of being the mysterious Madame Celestine who was never seen at social events... and she was about to risk it all for one dance in a moonlit garden.

This is madness, that sensible voice insisted. *You shouldn't!*

And she really shouldn't, Clara thought to herself.

"Thank you, my lady, but I must decline." Clara curtsied, gathering her sewing kit. "I have other appointments this evening."

But as she slipped out of the chamber and headed for the servants' exit, the glimpse of those moonlit gardens through every window she passed made her steps slow.

Just one peek couldn't hurt, could it? The gardens were technically outside the ball... and she'd always wondered what the famous Pembroke roses looked like up close...

No, no, absolutely not, she scolded herself, even as her feet carried her away into the gardens. She'd just take one quick look and return. As she rounded a corner to return to the house then—

"Oof!"

She collided with what felt like a wall of solid muscle, her sewing kit tumbling from her hands. Strong hands steadied her before she could fall, and she found herself staring up into the most striking green eyes she'd ever seen.

"My apologies," said a voice that sent shivers down her spine. "I wasn't watching where I was going."

Clara meant to step back. She really did. But those hands were still on her waist, and something about his half-smile made her feel wonderfully dizzy.

"Clearly not," she managed, proud that her voice came out steady. "Do you always lurk in doorways waiting to assault unsuspecting ladies?"

His eyebrows shot up, and that half-smile grew into something devastatingly charming. "Only on Tuesdays. And only the particularly intriguing ones who appear to be escaping the ball rather than entering it."

"I'm not escaping," she protested. "I'm... taking air."

"In the opposite direction of the gardens?"

Clara felt her cheeks heat. Thank goodness for the mask. "Perhaps I prefer my air without roses and judgmental gentlemen."

He laughed—a rich, warm sound that did dangerous things to her resolve. "Then allow me to make amends. The gardens really are spectacular, and I happen to be an excellent guide. Not judgmental at all, I promise."

Say no, that sensible voice screamed. *Leave now!*

"I shouldn't..." she began.

"Ah, but the best stories never start with 'I should,'" he pointed out, offering his arm.

And maybe it was the moonlight, or his smile, or the way this whole evening felt like a dream anyway, but Clara found herself taking his arm.

"Just a brief tour," she stipulated.

"Of course." His eyes sparkled with mischief. "Though I should warn you—the gardens have a way of making time slip away."

As he led her down the moonlit path, Clara tried to remind herself of all the reasons this was a terrible idea. But with his warm hand covering hers on his arm, and the night air sweet with roses, those reasons seemed to slip away just as easily as time.

"I'm Eustace, by the way," he said softly.

"Charlotte," she lied, picking the first name that came to mind. She'd regret it later, but right now, in this moment, she just wanted to be someone else. Someone who could walk in moonlit gardens with handsome strangers without worrying about rent payments and reputations.

"Well, Charlotte," he smiled down at her, "shall we see if we can find some trouble to get into?"

Clara knew she should be scandalized by such a suggestion. Instead, she found herself laughing. "I thought you promised not to be judgmental?"

"I did. Which is why I'm not judging your clear desire for adventure."

"You know nothing about me."

"I know you're wearing a mask that cost someone many sleepless nights to create. I know you move like someone who's used to going unnoticed, yet you hold yourself like a queen. And I know that despite your protests, you're just as curious as I am to see where this evening might lead."

Clara's heart skipped. He was far too perceptive. "For someone not judging, you're making an awful lot of assumptions."

"Not assumptions. Observations." He paused by the fountain, turning to face her. "Dance with me?"

Music drifted from the ballroom, a waltz that made her feet itch to move. "There's no one else dancing out here."

"Precisely why we should."

Don't, that sensible voice begged. But Clara was already stepping into his arms, her heart racing as his hand settled on her waist.

After all, what was one dance in a moonlit garden? What could possibly go wrong?

Eustace was an excellent dancer. Of course he was.

Clara tried not to notice how perfectly they moved together, how his hand felt warm and sure against her waist, how his eyes never left her face.

"You're very quiet suddenly," he murmured, guiding her around the fountain.

"I'm concentrating on not falling into the water."

"I wouldn't let you fall." His voice had dropped lower, more intimate. "I suspect you rarely let anyone catch you though, do you?"

Clara's breath caught. He was far too perceptive, this stranger who wasn't really a stranger anymore. "You talk as if you know me."

"I'd like to."

The music from the ballroom changed then, shifting to a slower, more romantic melody that made her heart ache. Violins and piano intertwined in a way that seemed to echo the strange tension building between them.

"Come inside," Eustace said softly. "Dance with me properly."

"I shouldn't." But her protest sounded weak even to her own ears.

"Even mysterious ladies in masks deserve to dance sometimes." His thumb traced small circles on her hand. "Just one more dance. Inside, where I can see your eyes properly."

This is the stupidest thing you've ever done, her sensible side warned as she let him lead her toward the ballroom. *Stupider than the French accent. Stupider than—*

But then they were through the doors, and Clara forgot how to think entirely. The ballroom was a swirl of candlelight and color, hundreds of crystals in the chandeliers casting rainbow shadows across the floor.

Whispers followed them as Eustace led her to the center of the room.

"Who is she?"

"Have you ever seen her before?"

"Look how he's looking at her..."

Clara's heart thundered as Eustace pulled her close again. This wasn't like the garden. Here, under the bright lights and curious stares, everything felt more intense.

More real.

"Everyone's staring," she whispered.

"Let them." His hand slid slightly lower on her back, just shy of scandalous. "I can't blame them. You're the most interesting thing that's happened all season."

They moved together as if they'd been dancing for years. Each turn, each step perfectly matched.

Clara felt almost dizzy with it—the warmth of his hands, the scent of his cologne, the way the room seemed to fade until it was just the two of them.

"Tell me who you are," he murmured, his lips close to her ear.

"I can't."

"Can't? Or won't?"

She looked up at him then, a mistake. His eyes held hers, intense and searching, and something electric passed between them. He pulled her incrementally closer, their bodies now touching in ways that would definitely set tongues wagging.

"Both," she managed.

The music swelled, and Eustace spun her in a series of quick turns that left her breathless. As they turned, Clara caught glimpses of the crowd—wide eyes, pointing fingers, furious whispers.

And then—it happened so quickly—her mask caught on a button of his coat during a turn. She felt the ribbon give way before she could stop it.

Time seemed to freeze.

The mask fell.

Gasps echoed through the ballroom.

"My God," someone whispered. "It's her. It's Vittoria."

Clara's blood ran cold. Who?

But then she saw Eustace's face—the shock, the recognition, the flash of something else she couldn't name—and realized exactly who they thought she was.

The countess. His former fiancée.

Before she could speak, before she could move, before she could do anything to correct this horrible mistake, Eustace's voice rang out clear and strong:

"It seems the fates have decided to give us another chance, my dear."

The room erupted in excited chatter. Clara stood frozen, her heart pounding so hard she thought it might burst. This couldn't be happening. This wasn't—

But it was. And as Eustace lifted her hand to his lips, his eyes never leaving hers, Clara had one crystal clear thought:

I am in so much trouble.

Click here now to get Clara Stitched in Secrets! https://www.amazon.com/dp/B0DS56JPRT

Printed in Dunstable, United Kingdom